The
Cyspherion

The Painryte Chronicles:

Part One

Aaron M. Farley

Frosted Rob Productions

This is a work of fiction. All the characters and events portrayed in this novel are either fictitious or are used fictitiously.

THE CYSPHERION

ISBN: 978-0-6151-5965-2

Cover Art by Lindsey Beaudreau

Revised edition: August 2007

Frosted Rob Productions

Frosted7rob@yahoo.com

(401)-206-3896

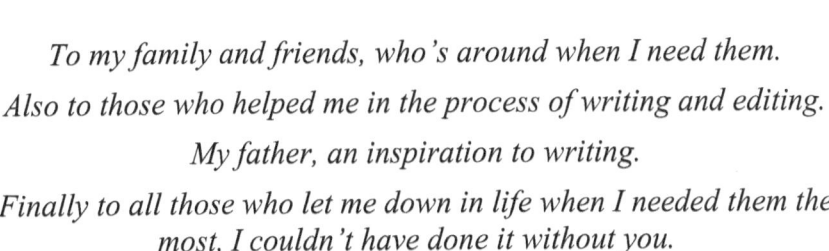

To my family and friends, who's around when I need them.

Also to those who helped me in the process of writing and editing.

My father, an inspiration to writing.

Finally to all those who let me down in life when I needed them the most, I couldn't have done it without you.

"I form the light, and create darkness: I make peace, and create evil: I the LORD do all these things." Isaiah 45:7

The
Cyspherion

Chapter 1

Casper braced against the cold rain as he walked down the street. A heavy sigh came from his lips as he slowed his pace considerably. Tired from his job, he thought back to earlier when he had just finished the day's work in a house cleaning service. More specifically, he moved junk out of old homes and palmed it off as antiques. Not exactly a dream job but he was in no position to enhance his life. Besides, he had known Jesse, his boss, since he could remember and they had become close friends over the years. Not that he minded his job, despite his boss working him harder then the rest of the group. He just grew weary of scamming naïve people out of their money. He couldn't complain about the conditions though as he was the only one working illegally in Jesse's company. Not existing in the government's eyes, he had no legal background and had to settle for a shabby house on the edge of town rented out to him by a low-income family that didn't mind keeping his secret. The old house was paid for by working under the table for Jesse.

Living off the streets since birth, he had never met his real parents nor did he know anything about where he came from. The only plausible hint as to who he was came from matching tattoos inhumanely etched on his wrists, a constant reminder of false promises and hopeless dreams. They bore Christian Crosses engulfed in flames and surrounded with a giant C. Inside the cross was scrawled the name Michael and in the fire, Maverick. The I in Michael was encased in the C itself where it overlapped the cross. Standing off balance inside the C, it looked almost like a crooked pillar with the top and bottom containing sideways eights. The E in Maverick was done in a fancy format, making it more appealing than the rest of the word. Because these were undoubtedly important images of his past, those who found him dubbed him Casper Michael Maverick. But despite being part of his history, he abhorred these markings.

The cold wind and harsh rain snapped him out of the trance only to find himself clutching his wrists, concealing the writing underneath. As he moved his hands he looked down at the tattoos glistening in the rain. He studied their artwork blending in the rain drops. It made him smile a little as rain often comforted Casper. He never understood why people ran through without stopping to enjoy it. For him the rain meant solitude and he always felt the best when he was away from society. With the cool water blurring out the tattoos, it almost made him feel like he was someone else. Never being told who he was often bothered him but without knowing where to start looking he had to settle for just being Casper, the Nobody.

The rain accompanied his hollow feelings. Licking his lips slowly, he could feel a salty taste on them as the water mixed with tears on his stern face. He seldom cried and never in another's company. The streets made him strong and he let no emotions escape to the outside world. But the streets cursed Casper and what made him strong was his weakness. While walking through the town he couldn't help but envy those families framed within windows and shades.

These thoughts had made Casper pause but a fresh blast of air reminded him of his surroundings. He had stopped right outside of a dark alleyway near his house. Listening closely, he thought he heard the sounds of a familiar voice drifting out from the back street, calling his name. The sounds died out before he could summon the courage to venture down to find out who was making them. It wasn't safe in this part of town he thought. Peering back around, he drew his trenchcoat closer and quickened his pace home and away from the strange alley.

"Home," Casper whispered. At least now he had a place to go with a roof and walls. A place he could finally call his own. Too deep in his own thoughts, Casper never heard the wet footsteps following only a stone's throw away.

*C*hapter 2

Sunlight fought its way through the grimy windows to rest upon Casper's face. The dull brightness made him squint until, slowly, the room came into focus. His gaze rested on the alarm clock by his couch, reading 7:25. "Damn," he muttered pulling himself off the torn furniture. He was already half an hour late for work.

Groggily glancing around the room he let the sleep clear his head and then glared back at the clock. He watched the minute switch up to 7:26 before grabbing it, and using it like a ball, threw it against the wall. A violent shower of pieces was evidence enough that the equipment would never work again. "Why do you do this to me?" He roared at its remains as they fell onto the floor. The only response was the faint sound of a radio station as the capacitors gave their last electric discharge.

Casper ran out of the house without bothering to change. He was glad that he had fallen asleep with clothes on that vaguely resembled work clothes and didn't need to worry about being any later from any delays. His demeanor turned to slight irritation as he now found himself jogging down the street, a form of exercise he was definitely not fond of. He felt a person should be able to get to one place from another with walking or driving and anything else should be considered crude and undignified. There were exceptions to this rule, of course. One exception was being late for work, which was his current situation and the other was running from the long arm of the law.

Being an Orphan from the streets, Casper was no stranger to the police officers and dodging their watchful eyes became a constant practice. He was caught only once in the nearby town of Ravenport and spent a night in their rather damp jail cells. He found their services unsatisfactory and was only capable of leaving through persuasion of his usual, forceful nature. Hiding in the deserts of Utah made escape easy, once free of the jail cell's stone walls. Since then, Casper has remained ever vigilant, watching for law enforcement. He had a record now and a cop would be more than willing to book him if he was caught.

This only served to remind Casper of who would most likely be waiting around the next corner. Her name was Alyssa and her profession was not encouraged by upper society. The strumpet had always claimed to be eighteen but everyone knew she couldn't be any older than fifteen. She had always taken a liking to Casper and had often offered him services free of charge, even through his constant rejections. She thought her persistence would one day pay off and he'd give in but she was sadly mistaken.

Staying in the same area to work everyday, she would annoyingly sidetrack him on his run to work. He banked a sharp right and ducked down the closest alley. Steps slowed just a bit as he took in the sight before him. Fresh blood stained the brick walls and seeped onto the ground, painting the alley like a horrid movie scene. Realization bluntly struck him that just outside this grotesque scene was where he had stopped the night before. He sighed in passing, a little happier that he had moved along the night before. No bodies littered the tight alley connecting the two streets so Casper rushed on. The only item left there was a large knife, plunged deep into the ground, with the handle depicting some fierce fiery scene. Casper had no time to look any closer, so brushed the incident off. Crime was not uncommon in the area, and even with the excessive blood and failure to cover the scene, it was no different then any other. The back alleyway was only a slight set back for Casper in his run but it still made him take one last look back, to the mournful scene. The momentary distraction caused him to run directly into the elderly gentleman standing on the sidewalk on the other side of the alley. Not passing up the chance, he snaked his hand into the man's coat in search of any belongings, a learned and appreciated reflex. With a flourishing rifle, he felt around without being detected until his fingers rested upon a cloth sack. A strange find indeed, but Casper was in too much of a hurry to dwell on the reasons for one's possessions and pocketed it in hopes it contained something of value before turning fully around.

Casper was not above pick-pocketing and often used it to get by when food was in short supply. He viewed it as a profession and those who perfected the art of stealing should use their skills to claim money, much like a dancer or an athlete. Not worried about who was in front of him, he did it to anyone he bumped into. His friends already understood his need for cash and would always return it if he accidentally stole from a friend. He did, however, take more precautions when picking pockets as it was a mistake he made in Ravenport that caused him a night in jail. Picking a police man's pocket is always a good way to end up as he did.

Facing forward, Casper sized up the man in front of him. He stood about six feet tall and stared Casper down with cold and deathly black eyes. Casper would have guessed the man to be around sixty but had aged wondrously as he bore no wrinkles or tell-tale signs of becoming old, aside from his long, silky white hair. He could even be construed as handsome despite his age. It made Casper take a step back in shock, but then quickly turned into irritation when he realized the stranger was peering curiously at Casper's wrists. This guy was not from his town and no doubt a drifter, looking to freeload off of his friends. Casper shouldered the man on his way by, while spitting out "Watch where you're going, old man. I have no time for the likes of you." the man regained his balance from the push with only a slight stumble. As Casper hurried off all he could feel was the cold stare of those cruel black eyes on the nape of his neck.

He felt it all the way to Jesse's home where his coworkers met everyday, but the roar of the box truck shook the feeling off of his neck. He sprinted to the driveway to where the truck was just backing up. With practiced ease, Casper leapt on to the back, unfastened the lock and squeezed himself nimbly into the back before Jesse was even done backing out of the driveway. Sighing with relief, he slammed the door down behind him and collapsed with his back against one of the worn out wooden truck walls. He was lucky enough not to miss the truck, just the daily meeting Jesse held before starting out. Panting out of breath from his cross town run, he drew together the strength to look around. Five workers sat in the back of the truck today, including himself. Someone was missing from their normal team. Even though small rays of light filtered through the crudely cut holes in the walls to outline the other's faces, Casper was too tired to make out who each one was. Unsatisfied, he merely settled for wheezing as he lowered his head down to his chest.

●~~~~~~~~~~~~●~~~~~~~~~~~~●

An hour had passed and Casper was feeling better. The long drive indicated that their job would be in a neighboring town. Living in a small city like Heresen, there were only two other towns close enough to travel to. Ravenport and

Faulkland stood only a few miles north and south of Heresen's city limits. Because of their secluded location in the center of Utah, the three towns often strived to do their business together.

With a fierce heat, the desert sun beat through the holes on the left side of the truck, making Casper grin in relief. They were heading south towards the town of Faulkland. Being in Ravenport always made him uneasy and was in no mood to work there after the morning he had. Peeking through the air holes he could make out the desert stretching out before him. The truck would be arriving in Faulkland soon and work would begin. Casper started to slowly drum his knuckles against the wall while he turned halfway around, addressing the rest of the workers. "What did I miss today?"

"Not much, we going to some woman's house. She lost it to foreclosure." The sound of Enrique's Hispanic voice confirmed that he wasn't the one missing from the team. "Oh, and Peter never showed up. Lucky you got to the truck in time, or we'd be short two people." Casper nodded slowly. So Peter was out today. It was a pity. He was one of the strongest on the team and they really could have used him to move the big furniture that would most likely be waiting for them. It was unlike Peter to not show up for work. Concern slowly crept along his face as he thought of the blood stains in the alleyway. Peter lived nearby Casper and was never a likable fellow with all the neighbors. Often getting into arguments with them, he avoided all of the people around him except Casper.

"Don't worry, Casper. He called and told Jesse he was sick, had to go to the Ravenport Hospital." The sound of George made Casper spin on his heels to look towards the crouched figure. "He won't be in to work tomorrow either."

"Well what's wrong with him?" Casper asked, softening his face. Being sick was much better than being stabbed to death with a knife.

"I don't know," George replied. "It's like pneumonia or something. Jesse said he sounded terrible." Casper sighed and looked back out his peek hole. They were finally coming into Faulkland and Casper could already see the houses on the outer limits of the town.

As the truck came to a steady stop, the kickback assured Casper and the other movers that they were at their destination. The door of the truck flew up, revealing Jesse's staunch figure. His face turned from disappointment to relief as a grin spread across his face. "Ah Casper, decided to show up then?" Jesse exclaimed. "I thought you'd be just taking the day off on us."

"Why would I be doing that, boss?" asked Casper as he jumped down.

Jesse's eyes narrowed down to slits. "You weren't at our meeting this morning. By the rules of the company I shouldn't even let you work."

Looking forward, Casper walked by him and merely replied with, "Yeah, but boss, I'm out of money, and I'm in need of a new alarm clock. I'm sure you can let it slide just one day." Jesse twisted his thick neck to watch Casper walk by without saying a word. He was tempted to make Casper take the day off as was the company's policy, but he couldn't afford to be missing two people and not having Peter was bad enough.

The other four workers jumped down and lined up outside on the sidewalk. Casper stared at the house as the rest of them walked up next to him. A beautiful old house three stories high stood proudly before them. Casper could tell this house was worth quite a bit if someone just fixed it up. Whoever was losing this gem had a terrible hand in fate. Hearing muffled sobbing, Casper's eyes shifted over to the lady sitting on the steps leading up to the house itself. It must be the woman who used to own this magnificent house, Casper thought to himself. The old lady seemed to be unmoving save her face, buried deep in her hands, which moved slowly back in forth. A pang of sorrow in his gut let Casper know this was not going to be an easy job today. Looking back, he saw Jesse talking to a man in a business suit. His appearance led him to believe that the aging man was from the bank and responsible for Jesse's deal with the furniture removal. The five workers walked by to stand by Jesse and await orders. Looking up, the banker realized that he and Jesse were no longer alone.

"Ah, you must be the home cleaners then?" the balding banker asked rhetorically. Pausing in a professional manner, he cleared his throat a moment before continuing. "Your job is in this despicable white house before you." The banker used his facial features as well as his thumb to point disdainfully in the direction of the house and as he did so, the old lady caught his attention. "Don't let that old crow bug you. If she was that attached to the house, she would've made her payments on time."

Casper knew better than to open his mouth but at the pathetic sight of the old lady, he found he couldn't help himself. "Couldn't you have given her more time? I mean, I don't think she means you any harm and was probably trying everything in her power to make her payment." The combined glare of anger from Jesse and the banker made him realize that his sympathy was lost on them and there was nothing to be said to them that could help the lady. After what felt, at least to Casper like forever, the banker made his reply.

"You know, I'm tired of everyone making me out to be the bad guy, the enemy. I do my job and I do it well. She got a loan from us, promising to pay it and now she can't. In return, we take her house. That's how the business world works, son. Now if you'll be so kind as to do your job, we'll be back in business. Or is that too hard for you to understand?" Reprimanding Casper in such a fashion was never a good idea. If this was to occur anywhere else, the banker would not have gotten a whole sentence out before hitting the ground in response to Casper's fist. But since he was working and this man was just another client, violence would solve nothing. Hitting him would cost Casper his job and possibly a trip to Faulkland's Jails. Keeping this in mind, he merely sank his head downwards and barely uttered an "Understood," just under his breath.

The group walked grudgingly towards the house with Casper trailing behind. He paused on the stone stairs just outside the house to look at the ragged form of the former home owner. The poor woman must have been even older then her house was. They had both weathered the years but from the looks of it, the house was doing a better job at withstanding time. For just a moment he contemplated comforting her and his hand slowly started to drop, as if to rest on her wiry white hair. A call from Jesse, who now stood impatiently at the door, snapped Casper out of the trance and he hurried to the door, passing Jesse without looking at him. He couldn't bear to meet the glare in Jesse's eyes.

The slam of the door behind him alerted Casper that Jesse was indeed not pleased with his actions. At least he had a full day of work ahead of him and the more he worked, the less Jesse could reprimand him. He walked into the left side of the house and into the living room where everyone was congregating for further orders. Upon passing a window, Casper peered out to see the banker confronting the elderly lady. From the look on his face, he knew the banker was not being kind with his words. The heartless man walked away contented and Casper watched the woman pick herself up and slowly move over to the sidewalk, where she collapsed and continued her sorrowful crying. Casper's heart stung more than ever. Even as a stranger to the lady, he knew this was no way to treat a human, especially a senior like her. A firm hand slapped down on Casper's shoulder, startling him back to attention as his reflexes made him turn around.

Chapter 3

Casper spun in alarm and met Jesse's cold stare. Too late for him to avoid it, the two were locked in a gaze. Only then did Casper see the pain in his eyes. Hidden under years of faithful service to the company his father had created for him was the true feelings Jesse had always felt. He never felt right with what he did, but couldn't let his father down. He had always pressured Jesse to succeed and even after his death, Jesse still felt his father's cold words from the grave, forcing him forward toward his twisted success.

This only took a moment, but in that time Casper was flooded with Jesse's emotional tidal wave. He suddenly understood why Jesse kept in business. It was not for himself, but for the love of his father. He never knew what it was like to feel the love of a father as his was too busy working to spend time with him. The only way he felt he could fix his past was to continue in his dad's footsteps. These feelings shook Casper to the bone, for he didn't know where they were coming from nor did he understand how Jesse's past revealed itself to him in such a vivid way.

"Get back to the group," Jesse said softly, breaking the silence. "We'll talk later." Casper wondered if Jesse had experienced the vision with him, but unable to even mouth out the question, he settled for a sigh. As he walked silently back to stand next to George in the group, he saw a faint flash of black cloth from the corner of his eye. With a quick twist, he turned quickly to focus in on it, but it had already vanished. He grunted and decided the day was wearing away on him and his eyes were starting to see things.

"Listen up people, we've got just today to move everything out of this old house and onto the truck. This means we'll be working hard and we'll be taking limited breaks." The crew grumbled in acceptance and each worker was given their assignment of work. Casper was paired up with George and they were starting on the third floor, in the bedroom, while Chuck and Noah tackled the second floor. Because Peter was missing, Jesse was forced to team up with Enrique and they took the first floor. He claimed this was because the most valuable possessions were located on the first landing but everyone realized it was because the first floor was the easiest part of the job.

Casper climbed the stairs and even though he was close behind George, the spiraling staircase made it hard to keep sight of him. He could hear George's garbled curses floating throughout the staircase and added some of his own. It would be hard enough to move everything out of the house, but the staircase's spiraling architecture would only impede their work. In silence, they shared pleas that all the bulky furniture would be downstairs and not in their territory. Passing though the stairwell, Casper noted fresh markings along the walls. Something big had passed through here recently and whoever moved it was not being careful with it.

At the top of the stairwell, George waited for Casper just outside the bedroom door, where they would be starting their work. Both men took in a deep breath as Casper's hand slipped onto the door knob. Slowly twisting it, they heard the screeching of a bolt in dire need of oil. He pushed the door inwards and as it swung open, the groaning hinges rung in the still air. Holding their breath, Casper and George walked into the almost vacant room to look around. Their biggest fear, the bed, was missing and all that remained where it once stood was a patch of discolored flooring, roughly bed shaped. Letting out a sigh of relief, Casper and George circled the room to examine what little furniture was left in the dimly lit room.

"I hope all of our rooms are like this," George said as he knelt on the barren floor, taking a closer look at the patch of discolored wood. "She must have sold the bed to help pay off her loan." Casper merely nodded, walking over to an old, well built desk. Of all the furniture scattered about the room, it looked the most promising as an antique. Possibly the first and only genuine antique Jesse will ever get his hands on, Casper thought to himself.

As he ran a hand over it and pushed away the ancient dust, he was surprised at the smoothness. Not even a dent reflected on its immaculate surface. Upon closer inspection, he realized there was a small area on the surface of the desk where the dust had collected less than on the rest of the surface. Casper pressed his hand firmly on the area and the wood gave way under the pressure. It spun over and stood perpendicular to the desk itself. A decorated nail was carefully driven into the slab of wood but what caught Casper's attention was hanging from the nail. A gold necklace, accented with silver and diamonds, was crafted into a Celtic knot and hung on from the desk, suspended by its golden chain.

Casper turned slightly to see that George was now looking through a standing wardrobe, looking for valuables no doubt. Turning back to the desk, Casper carefully relieved the nail of its burden and drew it to his face for closer inspection. He turned it over and over in his palm, concentrating solely on its workmanship. A note was attached on the knot and as it fluttered slowly on the chain, he became aware of it. He grabbed it with one hand and read words off of the old piece of paper. Written in very fine print, Casper could barely make out what it said, but mouthed the words as he read them to himself.

To my Dearest,

May spirits keep us together.

Our hearts are bound in this knot.

Never lose this, or Lost is our Love.

Your Love, AMF.

Casper read this note over and over, wondering what it meant. "What've you found, anything of value?" George asked from the wardrobe, breaking Casper's concentration. Casper shook his head as he quickly plunged the knot into his pocket, next to the cloth sack he had pocketed earlier.

George looked at him in an unconvinced snarl, but knew better then to pry. The unsaid rule of the workers was that if anything turned up of any value that could be snuck past Jesse, it was theirs to keep. Casper watched George for a minute, judging his reaction. He knew George saw some part of the necklace. "Let's open the window. It's as hot as hell in here." George said with a flourish of his hands, pretending he didn't care about the findings.

Casper shuffled over to the window and after releasing the latch, saw the sight taking place on the street. The old woman who once owned the house was now standing near Jesse's truck, distraught about something. The banker was back, evidently confronting her once again. Jesse and Enrique were on the sidewalk, carrying a rather heavy looking table. Lifting up the window, Casper could hear the dispute below.

"Not the table, please, not the table." The old woman sobbed. "My husband built it himself with his own bare hands for me. It was the last gift I ever received from him."

"Listen Carol dear. You signed an agreement. If you failed to pay, which you did, we take the house and everything in it. I want to hear no more of this. I can and will call the police force if you continue." The banker, proud of himself, pulled a phone out of his suit pocket, and waved it, as if to threaten her with it. The uncaring Carol ran behind the truck to block Jesse and Enrique as they approached the loading ramp. The banker grabbed her arm and threw her brutally back onto the sidewalk. "I've had enough of you and your sob stories!" he yelled. "Get in their way again and you'll be taking a trip downtown!" Satisfied that he had proven his point, the banker walked off, his portly shape waddling toward what Casper could only imagine was his car.

"Hey Casper, get over here. I can't move this on my own." Casper turned to see George examining the wardrobe for handholds. He quietly stepped over to the wardrobe and assumed a lifting position, squatting on his legs for balance and reached around the furniture in search for a hold and easily found holes to put his hands in. Both men ready, they lifted in unison and made their way to the door. The wardrobe fit perfectly down the stairs and out the front door without any problems. Casper kept his eyes off of the ragged pile that made up Carol as they staggered onto the sidewalk. He couldn't bear looking at her. The two of them placed the wardrobe carefully into the truck and headed back inside, followed by Carol's soft sobbing. As they walked back up the narrow steps, they reached the almost barren bedroom where they saw the desk once again. Casper and George carried it carefully down to the truck. Walking once again past the disheveled woman, Casper couldn't help but to wander his eyes over to where she was sitting. Carol looked up as a shock of panic radiated her body.

Her muscles tensed as if to lunge for the desk that once hid her secret. Just before she acted, her eyes darted to where Jesse was now standing. She relaxed and resumed the pathetic mass of woman on the side of the street. Casper winced slightly at her actions.

Casper followed George once again up the stairwell and into the bedroom. "Well," George started. "That looks like it for this room. Why don't you go to the room on the left and I'll search the room to the right?"

Casper looked back out into the hallway and agreed silently. Walking toward his destination, he wondered what other treasures he might find in this old house. Once he approached the doorway, he examined the worn door only to find no door knob. He rested one hand against the wood and pushed. The panel swung forward and a darkened storage space stood before him. Glancing back, he saw George entering the door on the opposite side of the hall.

Breathing in the musty air about him, Casper walked into the small area. All that occupied the space was a stool and a standing mirror. He dropped his body onto the stool as he realized how tired he had been. Sleep had evaded him the night before, leaving him deprived of rest. His birthday was in two days and he would be turning twenty one yet he had still not fulfilled his childhood dreams of changing the world, ending poverty, and giving everyone a place to belong. Leaning back against the wall, he heard a dull thud of something hitting the floor. Looking down, he realized the cloth sack had fallen free of his pocket. George would surely be busy for some time, no doubt searching every crevice for a trinket or two to make ends meet in his budget. Casper had some time to himself.

He picked up and rolled the red bag in his hand, taking time to appreciate the soft fabric. Not an expert on cloth, he assumed it was made of velvet. Turning it over displayed a peculiar name, embroidered with gold thread. "Wyburn,"

Casper sounded off, letting the strange name roll throughout his mouth. After he felt satisfied with the sound of the name, he turned his attention back to the bag. What was important to Casper was not the bag itself, but what the bag held. He carefully inched open the drawstring and emptied its contents onto an open palm.

What fell from its clothed prison was a metal ball. Casper brought it closer to his face for a better look, for the ball introduced a new curiosity to Casper. It was made of a strange white metal so bright that it seemed to radiate its own glow. Curiosity turned into panic when Casper learned that the ball was no longer solid, but instead was melting in his very hand. No amount of shaking could release its grasp on Casper. As he gazed in amazement, the liquid metal slowly formed a haunting image in the palm of his hand. Barely able to breathe, he could only stand to stare at the insignia. The image captive in the metal was very similar to very the tattoos drawn on his own flesh. It contained a cross in the same fashion as Casper's, but where his flames were stood a giant set of wings surrounding the cross. Written in the cross was the name, Aspriel and where Casper's C was set, an A was written instead. Mesmerized by this scene, it took a moment for him to feel the warm gaze but as he looked up he found trapped within the mirror was a woman like none he had ever seen. She was too beautiful for words to ever describe. Her flowing snow-white hair waved in an unseen breeze while her green eyes made him feel at home. Perfection still fell short of this lady's face. Her lips moved with grace as she spoke.

"Michael, Michael," she repeated slowly. "Michael, you need to listen to me. You are in a terrible danger." Unable to reply, Casper merely stared back at the visage of heaven. "Heed my warnings, trust only in yourself."

The room started spinning and Casper was losing focus. Finally able to vocalize a response, a rush of questions flooded

Casper's mind. "Wait, who…who are you?" he asked. "Why are you calling me Michael?" Just as he was about to ask more questions, the room become dim and no longer clear, but a disturbing blur of colors.

"Seek out the Crosspien Vampyres. They will answer your questions and they will help you find yourself." These were the final words Casper heard as the room faded to complete darkness.

"So this is where you've been hiding?" Casper awoke from his sleep to find George standing over him. "I've had to move almost all my room down to the truck on my own and yet here you are, lounging around."

Casper jumped up with a start and looked around. The room was back in the same dismal shape he had entered it in. "Sorry George, I must have dozed off for a while," he answered while his attention was directed back toward the mirror's greasy surface, which only served to reflect Casper's piercing blue eyes. "I must be more tired than I thought," He added, "Come on, let's go move your room out."

George walked out of the room but took time to respond as he strode out. "It's all set, I'm done my room and we'll be taking our only break. Jesse wants to see you during lunch though." Casper watched George leave and then his thoughts returned to the strange metal from Wyburn's cloth sack. Searching the floor, he saw the ball of white only a few feet from his leg. Pulling the velvet bag inside out, Casper used it as a glove to scoop up strange metal. Even though he was certain it was only a dream brought on by pure exhaustion he was still shaken up and was taking no chances in touching the bizarre substance.

Walking back downstairs, he saw Jesse pacing the living room. When he motioned him over, he complied and found a bench that had not yet been moved out by Jesse or Enrique. He sat uncomfortably on the rough edge and leaned forward, waiting for Jesse's speech.

"Listen Casper," he began as his eyes darted around the room, "I know how you feel about work. It's not a very honest business and having to take the belongings from this poor woman is even worse, but think of the business." He leaned forward and braced his hand on Casper's shoulder, bringing his face close to his. "This furniture is the best I've ever seen and we'll be making a lot of money selling it off. Maybe I can give you guys all bonuses and buy a new truck. You know the trip here only takes twenty minutes and yet we needed over an hour." Jesse paused in his speech. Looking around at the remaining furniture, he started speaking his thoughts out loud. "I think these are genuine antiques." Casper turned his head away as Jesse paused another moment. "Come on Casper, forget about the lady. This is strictly business and we can't let emotions get in our way."

Casper sat silently for a minute. "Whatever you say, boss. It's your call, after all. She's got a name though, its Carol." He responded, as he got up and pushed past Jesse to head to the door.

"Where are you going?" Jesse called after him.

"To go eat lunch I'm starving," was his only reply before walking out of the house. Jesse watched him walk away and could almost feel tears come to his eyes. He never meant to hurt Carol, only live up to his late father's expectations.

Casper walked into the front yard and leaned against the iron fence bordering the lawn. His wandering gaze fell down upon Carol, who sat on the sidewalk, still a sobbing disgrace. He wondered what would become of her. Perhaps her family would take her in and let her live with them, but he doubted it. She looked lonely and Casper guessed any relatives of Carol had passed away. Feeling obligated, he made his way down onto the sidewalk and sat next to her. Oblivious to her new company, Carol continued crying. He moved his hand on her bony shoulder making her jump in surprise. She looked up sorrowfully to meet Casper's cool stare and relaxed a little.

"It's alright, my name's Casper. You had a beautiful house and I'm terribly sorry that ass from the bank is taking it from you." He cooed serenely in hopes to soothe her.

"This house is all I have left of my husband. I've sold everything in it to try and pay off the loan, but I just couldn't sell what belonged to him." She lowered her head as she coughed out reply. "I needed the loan to give him a proper funeral. It was the least I could do after all he did for me over the years. I thought I would be able to pay it off, but work…" Carol started sobbing softly again. "Work laid me off. They said I was getting too old to function properly. Now I have no where to turn and no reason to live." Carol's words cut through Casper's heart like a searing knife. He wrapped his arm around her small frame. Placing his arm onto her other shoulder, he drew her closer into a hug in attempts to calm her a little. Decisions weighed heavy on Casper, and it took him time before he could find the words to respond.

He finally spoke softly. "Well, you seem like a wonderful woman. Your husband must have been very lucky. I'm sure he was very fond of you and I think there is something he wants you to have." Questions filled her eyes as she looked back up at him. Tears glistened on her cheeks as she began to speak, but Casper cut her off as he motioned her to stay quiet. Reaching into his pocket, he pulled out the one possession she would be able to keep. The knot dangled from the chain as he strung the necklace around her neck in one fluid motion and smiled as she stared at him with amazement.

"Oh thank you, thank you so much," she stuttered, rubbing the necklace in disbelief. "I thought it would be lost forever. You must be my angel!" Casper tried to deny any claim to being an angel, but his protest was lost in Carol's warm embrace as she hugged him deeply. Casper knew he was no angel but it made the poor woman happy, so he did not see the harm in it. "I better leave, before that banker returns." she said, loosening her hold on Casper. "It was very nice meeting you. Oh thank you, thank you, and thank you." She repeated over and over as she pulled him close for one more even tighter hug. Releasing him, she stood and started walking down the street. Casper pushed himself to his feet and began his walk to the house. When he reached the fence, Casper started wondering where exactly she was going. Turning around, he saw that Carol was no where in sight. It was almost as if she had just disappeared. Spinning on his heel, Casper kicked the fence in anger. That necklace could have fed him and his friends for a month at the very least. He hated when emotions got in the way of his very survival.

Casper rested on a rugged chair in the back of the truck. The rest of the day went without incident. They had moved all of the furniture out in scheduled time and were now on their way back to Heresen. The absence of Carol had made work easier for Casper as he no longer felt sorrow for her. Her smile had shaken the feeling of anguish from his mind. The truck shook on the ill kept road bumping them about, but having furniture made the trip a little more pleasurable. Noah was sprawled across a table, half asleep. The second floor had the heaviest furniture so Chuck and Noah were completely out of energy and could barely muster grunts as they hit each bump.

The truck came to a rolling halt and a sharp left indicated that they were back at Jesse's house. Opening the hatch, they all slumped out of the back of the truck to where Jesse stood waiting to address them with the final meeting of the day.

"Good news," Jesse boasted. "We have no jobs tomorrow, so you can all take the day off." Enrique was heard groaning in the group. He had a wife and three children and was barely able to support them on a full pay check. Taking a day off would mean disaster for his bills. "Since Peter can't work tomorrow, I need help unloading the truck," he continued, directing his words this time at Enrique. "Anyone who needs the extra hours can come and help me unload." Enrique sighed in relief, glad to be able to have his hours back. "Everyone have a good weekend and I'll see you all on Monday." he finished. The group dispersed and each one started their way home.

Shaken up by the day's events, Casper walked slowly through the streets. It had been an eventful day and his head was clouded with thoughts of the day's happenings. His mind centered on the dismal alleyway painted with blood when he reached his neighborhood. Out of interest, he made his way back to the deserted alley to inspect the scene. Shockingly, the area remained untouched as no one must have seen, or at least reported it to police. Crouching down, he examined the dried blood. He could tell whoever was wounded struggled and gave quite a fight, but was no match for the attacker. Turning over to the knife, he was surprised to find that it had cut straight through the concrete without snapping. The blade was made of a curiously strong and dangerously sharp alloy. Casper couldn't think of any kind of metal that could manage that feat.

Mesmerized by the knife's incredible strength, he couldn't stop himself as he slid his palm along the grip, which was fashioned in a hellish fashion. A fire burned fiercely in the picture, showing pictures that he could only interpret as eternal damnation. Attempting to free the blade from the ground, Casper heard a haunting voice behind him before the knife even moved.

"The assassin made a mistake," the voice stated. "Alyssa met a fate meant for you. You're lucky to be alive." He once again felt the cold black eyes on his neck again. Without turning around, he knew it was the old man from the morning, Wyburn.

Casper knew better than to stay around. His hand rested on a murder weapon and he had stolen a bag from Wyburn. Explanation to the police would be impossible and he had no intentions of going back to jail. Jumping up, he sprinted out of the alley and into the opposite street.

"Michael wait, we have to talk, you're not safe!" Hearing Wyburn's protests made him run even faster. He had learned the streets better than anyone in town, so knew he could easily lose the outsider in its mazes. Without looking, Casper ran into the road before he heard the car approaching. Without bothering to slow down, he rolled across the hood of the oncoming vehicle and landed safely on the sidewalk. Turning back, he couldn't see anyone following him. He thought it best to not slow his pace as Wyburn was still out there somewhere.

Wyburn had used Casper's middle name just like the mirage in the mirror did. Alyssa was dead and it was probably his fault. He wondered how Wyburn knew about him and the murder. These thoughts made him question how safe he was in town, making him run all the way home, feeling insecure about every person he passed. He never slowed his pace until he was at his house, to where Justine was waiting.

Chapter 4

Morning woke Casper to a new day. Tired and confused from his encounters, he had fallen asleep shortly after entering the house the night before. Hunger hit him as he remembered he hadn't eaten anything in two days. Trudging over to the battered refrigerator, he began to search for sustenance until the sound of Justine moaning interrupted him. His house was a safe haven for any of the desolate souls on the street, but he still preferred to know who inhabited his house while he was there.

Considering that Justine was just beginning to wake up, he knew she had spent the night there. He turned back to his search for food. Justine knew Casper better than any other person. She was there the night he was found and took an instant bond to the infant. Not having any children of her own, she had claimed him as her own son. Though only twelve at the time, she was the closest person to a mother Casper ever knew. Justine acted more of a friend or a sister then a mother to Casper and was constantly joking around with him. He heard her stir on the couch near him as the sounds from the kitchen woke her.

"Shouldn't you be at work, Justine?" Casper inquired, still rummaging through what little edibles he possessed.

"Shouldn't you?" she shot back. "I walked out of work yesterday. Ben pushed it way too far, and I couldn't take it anymore."

"I guess that means you won't be buying dinner tonight," Casper grumbled, slightly irritated. As long as they had known each other, Ben and Casper never got along. As civil as they were in public, it was clearly understood that there was a definite distaste between the two. Ben was the manager of a shipping dock for a local warehouse and Justine had been working for him. Ever since Justine had started working there, Ben hounded her for a date. It had started out as harmless gestures, but as the years progressed, he became more abrasive and blunt. Feeling overly protective of Justine, Casper would never pass up a chance to destroy Ben's face with his bare knuckles. What stopped him from fighting was the knowledge that Ben carried twin handguns engraved with his name. Ben wasn't afraid to use them and Casper knew he could never get close enough to do harm before he would be punctured with a bullet.

"So hey, why aren't you working?" Justine asked, sitting up and pushing her disheveled blonde hair out of her face.

"No jobs today. Jesse gave us the day off." he replied as he settled on some suspicious looking sliced ham and carried it over to where Justine was sitting. Dropping himself onto the couch, he took the seat next to Justine and offered her some of the spoiling meat. Leaning forward, Justine inspected the ham but scrunched her nose before getting too close.

"Hey, I think your ham's gone bad. You should throw it out," She advised, backing away from it. He brought the ham close to his face, sniffing the slightly foul odor for a moment.

Looking back at Justine, he smiled, took an unnecessarily large bite and replied with "Taste's fine to me and I've got no cash for food right now." His speech was muffled as he chewed the ghastly ham. "If you want food, go buy some yourself."

Justine closed one eye half way and glared at Casper while he ate, then spoke up. "I don't need to go buy food, I'll just help myself." He turned, but before he could object, Justine lunged forward and latched her jaw on Casper's neck. Wincing slightly, he could feel her sharp teeth as she ground them against his skin.

"Hey, get off me. I told you before, no biting! What the hell do you think you are a damn vampire?" Casper growled as he pushed her away. She flailed her arms but missed Casper's long black hair as she slid off the couch and hit the ground. The bite on his neck made Casper remember the memories of yesterday's events and as he rubbed the bite marks, he heard words pour out of his mouth. "Have you ever heard of a guy named Wyburn?"

Justine lay limp of the floor, rolling the name around in her mouth and combing her memory. "No, should I have? Is it someone important?" She questioned, sitting up to look at Casper from her seat on the threadbare rug.

"No, It was some guy I ran into on the street yesterday," Casper replied. "He generously offered this over to me." The cloth sack was pulled out of his pocket and into her sight.

Justine's focus centered on the item in his hand. She knew the sack wasn't given to him but wasn't about to protest Casper's methods of feeding him or herself, especially since she was now out of a job.

"Let me see what you got, you little miscreant," she joked. Casper shot a glance down at the spunky girl and nonchalantly threw the sack at her before he leaned his head back against the couch and dangled a piece of ham above his mouth. Justine, being less than agile, missed the catch and was forced to fetch it from behind her. "Looks worthless, a piece of pewter perhaps," she called up after a minute. This response made him drop the ham on his face and vault his torso forward to give Justine his full attention. The slice of ham on his face was flung forward, falling into Justine's uncombed hair.

"Ugh, can't throw a bag, but you've got good aim with ham." She snapped in disgust while peeling the meat out of her hair and flinging it away. He paid her actions no mind though. His eyes focused solely on the metal ball in Justine's hand. It no longer glowed white or melted, but shone a dull grey color on its surface. Justine turned back to the ball which she began to roll playfully between her hands. "It's pretty smooth," she claimed. "But it's definitely a cheap metal." He started to crawl off the couch and towards Justine's hand while her attention was drawn back to the other item she held. "I really like this bag, though" she smiled.

She was too distracted to see him paying attention to the metallic ball, which Casper watched change color. It dissolved from a dull grey back to a white shine in response to his approach. He drew back in horror, attracting the eyes of Justine.

"Can I have the bag?" she asked girlishly.

Casper shook his head, still in shock. The ball had returned to a dull grey, pewter like material. "Put it back in the sack," He answered quickly. Justine, disappointed, returned the ball to its holding bag as her smile disappeared. She harshly threw the velvet bag back at Casper, striking him in the chest. He grunted, catching the bag as it rolled down his chest and pocketing it with a flash.

Justine inched her way back onto the couch, next to Casper. "I need a place to stay." Her girlish tone returned as she played with his hair. He knew she was implying that she wanted to stay with him.

"What's wrong with your apartment?" he queried, moving over to give Justine her seat back.

"My rent is past due," she answered quickly. "Besides, Ben's going to show up there, I just know it. Please?" She begged.

"Fine, I'll make up the guest bed," he joked, getting up and grabbing a pillow from a nearby chair. Turning, he aptly tossed it onto the arm of the couch. He walked back over to her, smirking with content. "There, all set." The couch creaked as he sunk back into his seat. Justine glared at Casper in a mock anger, then leapt over and threw her arms around his body, giving him a silent thank you hug. Casper, in no mood to argue, just lay there and enjoyed the embrace.

Their embrace somehow turned into a wrestling match as the day progressed. One had moved and discomforted the other, beginning the fight. Rolling all around the furniture and floor, the bout ran on until the sun began to set. Breaks punctuated rounds by treaties called by a losing contester. Each one took its turn to attack the unsuspecting combatant soon after a treaty had been called. The lengths of these treaties varied from minutes to hours, depending on how long each one needed to take a break.

"Alright, I give up, I swear this time!" Casper yelled into the ground. Justine had finally pinned him face down and was bending his right arm behind his back. Letting go of her grip, she slowly let Casper get off the ground. At the first opportunity he launched an attack on Justine, yelling a war cry and pinning her to the ground. She furiously wrestled him off of her and they locked in a mutual grip. Realizing the predicament they were both in and how tired they had become, the two friends released their grip on each other and shared a laugh. The sound of a loud knocking at the door stopped them short. Looking at each other, they sat patiently until they heard the sound again.

"Get in back and hide." Casper said sharply, rising from the ground. He brushed himself off and headed for the door while Justine ducked down near the back of the small house. Reaching the door, he pulled it easily from the doorjamb to find Ben standing on the other side. A sudden tension filled the air that could be pierced with a sharp knife.

Ben broke the silence. "Where is she? I know she's here."

"What are you talking about?" Casper shot back. He knew he could take Ben easily and was always ready for a fight.

"Justine, she came here today. I need to talk to her, let me in." he demanded as he began to push his way into Casper's house.

Casper grabbed Ben's arm and forced him back. "What the hell do you think you're doing? This is my house, get out!" he yelled, pushing the forceful cretin back.

Ben was no longer thinking about Justine though. As he suddenly caught sight of Casper's raised wrist, his eyes were instantly drawn to them. Casper had always kept his wrists hidden from the world whenever possible, ashamed of his mysterious marks. It suddenly occurred to him that Ben had never seen his tattoos and was experiencing them for the first time. Gazing in wonder, he was only able to mutter one word.

"Cyspherion…" Both men's eyes turned back to stare at each other and Casper saw the amazement on Ben's face. He took this momentary shock as an advantage. Enraged at the sight and actions of Ben, Casper planted his foot into Ben's chest, forcing him backwards off of his porch steps while yelling down, "I told you, get off my porch!"

He jumped down next to Ben and assumed a fighting stance. Ready to throw the first blow, Casper was stopped short as Ben reeled around. Ben had taken one of his side arms out of its holster and turned around, burying the barrel end deep into Casper's neck. Breathing heavily, he stared down at the instrument of death, about to end his very life.

"My boss is really going to like this. I'll be handsomely rewarded for killing the cyspherion." his blank stare made Ben pause in mid speech. "You have no idea, do you? Well I'm not letting you live long enough to find out." Casper watched his mouth as it was drawn up into a grin.

"I don't think you're man enough to pull the trigger," Casper said slowly, stalling while he searched for a way to escape the situation. "I bet you can't even use that," he looked behind Ben, to where a cat was lying about and pointed his finger toward the creature as it purred in its nap by the side of the road. "I bet you couldn't even hit that fur ball from where you're standing." Ben's grin grew even wider. Without so much as looking, he pulled the matching gun from the confines of its holster and cocked it. Spinning it around gracefully in his hand, he took aim and made a blind shot behind him to where the unsuspecting animal was still sleeping. Following the gun's explosion, a dying screech was heard up and down the street. Casper saw the bloody mass convulse and lie still.

"Well what do you know, I think you were wrong." Ben replied as he brought his hand back to his face. "Any last words, Mr. Maverick?" the despicable man sneered as he rested the second gun on Casper's neck, parallel to the first.

Casper swallowed deeply, realizing he had only made the situation worse for himself and caused an innocent creature to die.

"Looks like I'm going to go join Fluffy over there," he gulped, trying to be smart, even in his dying moments. Closing his eyes, he held his breath and braced for imminent death. He could feel Ben slowly tightening forefingers around the triggers, savoring the moment. Casper wanted to fight back, but terror paralyzed him and he could do nothing but stand rooted in place and lose control of his breath as it escaped fiercely from his lungs. Casper never heard a gun shot but felt a burning sensation on his neck, accompanied with a blinding white flash knocking Casper backward a step. Dying was not the way Casper imagined it. Thoughts of how death should feel ravaged Casper's shredded thoughts, as his uncontrollable breathing slowed down considerably.

Chapter 5

The scent of scorched skin reached Casper's nose. Smelling the singed flesh, he slowly became aware that he was not dying. A burning sensation tore across his neck where the guns had been just moments before. In shock, he opened his eyes to the scene before him. Ben was stooping in Casper's front lawn to collect his handguns from where they had fallen. Taking a quick shot, he turned around and fired both guns in Casper's direction. He rolled nimbly to the side and narrowly averted the bullets as they found homes in the porch's woodworks. Ben glanced down the street before running off with a new look of terror on his face. As Casper followed his gaze, a feeling of nausea tore through him. Wyburn held his palm straight out as he walked up the street towards the house. When the old man lowered his hand, Casper thought a small puff of smoke wafted up from the hand. A quick decision led him to believe that standing around would be a poorly chosen action if he didn't want to die. Spinning back towards the house, he bolted up the porch steps and burst through the front door, exciting Justine.

"Is everything alright?" she asked, jumping up without thinking.

"Yeah it's just an old friend of mine. He's going to meet us over at the bar," he lied. "Let's go."

She began walking towards the front door but stopped short when Casper threw his arm out to block her path. "No take the back exit, its better." he snapped, "Hurry up."

She began to protest, but changed her mind when he grabbed up his knife. She instantly knew trouble was in the air. It was a six inch blade Casper never took anywhere unless there was clear and present danger. Sliding the piece of metal safely into his belt, he pushed the little spunky blonde towards the back window. Hoisting her up, Casper pushed her through before climbing out himself. The sun had almost fully set on the dirty alley just outside. As the two emerged from the window, the town's lights started to flicker on. Even with the limited lighting, he could tell they were alone behind his house. He motioned for Justine to stay low as they made their way between the refuse that littered the realms forgotten by those who took money for granted. Peeking around the corner of his house, he could barely make out the image of Wyburn holding the carcass of the cat Ben had just shot at.

Not wasting time to ponder what the old man was doing, Casper grabbed hold of Justine's wrist and pulled her forward into shadows that would wrap them in a secure blanket of invisibility. Vacating the premises, he felt a warm feeling that he could only surmise as love permeate the air as he ran off with Justine.

Casper and Justine ducked through the side streets until their favorite area of destitution came into view. It was a bar called Beezel's, where no one knew your name and a person could hide their history in a pitcher of cold liquor.

Walking up to the front of Beezel's, he blew a sigh of relief. Safety lay inside as long as their tab was paid. An easy target stumbled on the curb, a man too drunk to function properly in his surroundings. Casper walked up to him and frisked the drunkard for cash while Justine stood guard. The man, having consumed too much alcohol, believed Casper was the police and he was under arrest. As he searched for money, the drunk murmured about doing nothing wrong and not wanting to go to jail. Finding a cache of cash, he pushed the guy off and into the street, glad to have his pungent breathe away from him. He motioned back to Justine and they ducked down into Beezel's. Just before entering the dismal building, he paused to hear the distant baying of hounds echoing throughout the city. They were on the hunt in the barren deserts of Utah.

Casper's eyes adjusted to the dim bar. The room somehow made outside seem bright as day. Walking through the bar room, he couldn't avoid breathing in the fumes of extinguished cigars, even though he tried. He paused and surveyed the surroundings. Justine, realizing she was now walking alone, turned around to find Casper unconsciously fingering the knife concealed beneath his shirt while searching for any possibly hostile enemies.

"Keep it in your pants," she whispered, walking back to where Casper stood. He snapped his hand away from the knife and followed her over to a table. They looked down in disgust. What once was a table now loosely resembled a wooden structure coated in unknown matter left from years of poor cleaning habits. Taking a look around, they realized this table was in better condition then the others and settled for it as a resting point.

Casper slid himself into one of the chairs as Justine ventured her way over to the bartender. He ran his hand across the table only to give up when his hand stuck to the surface. Sighing, he closed his eyes and leaned his chair back on two legs. He tried to clear his mind of all the happenings of the previous few days. He preferred the life he had come to understand, where the streets wrote the rules and he enforced their will. The room melted away and fatigue started to claim Casper. What little ham he had eaten was not enough to sustain him for much longer and without nourishment, he had very little energy to concentrate. His thoughts blurred as pangs of hunger set in. Just in time, he heard a plastic dish slam down on the table. Pushing his chair forward while snapping open his eyes, he was met with a bowl of onion rings drenched in grease and barely recognizable, just the way Casper liked them. Without consent, he began wolfing down the greasy rings. Rings dangled from his mouth as he paused a moment to look at Justine who was sitting down across from him.

"Drink?" he demanded, impatiently raising an eyebrow.

Justine laughed at Casper's actions before sliding a beer across the table to him. The bottle skidded on the sticky surface and started to tip. The table shuttered as he lunged for the beer and grabbed it from the table. Justine watched him greedily gulp down the cheap alcohol before speaking.

"A little hungry are we?" she asked. "Guess that ham didn't cut it?" He looked up for a second and shook his head vigorously, then continued stuffing rings in his mouth, stopping only to wash it down with his beer.

Amused by the young man's actions, she had forgotten her food and how she hadn't eaten in some time. A growl of her stomach reminded her and she clutched it while grunting slightly. This caught Casper's attention. Looking up, he used his head to motion towards her bowl of french fries, implying that she should eat the grease infested potato shards. Grabbing the bottle of ketchup from the side of the table, she opened the top and dumped the red ooze into her bowl to add taste to the grisly food. Grabbing a handful of fries, she slathered them into the ketchup before stuffing them into her open jaws.

"You know what? We always come here and yet the food never gets better." Justine noted after a few pieces of the wretched fries. "You'd think they could hire better cooks with the business they get from us."

"Well at least it's cheap and better than what's left at my house," he answered between bites of the onion rings. With a curious eye, he looked up to watch Justine as she fiddled with her bottle of beer, rolling it between her hands as she thought alone to herself. Drawing the bottle up to her lips, she took a big swig and swallowed the fluid with a loud gulp.

"Well big guy," she said before letting out a large belch. "Tomorrow you're going to be able to buy this all on your own." He snorted politely at her joke. They both knew Casper could and had been buying alcohol for the past five years. The bartender Noel knew Casper and never asked him for any identification. He had just always assumed that Casper was old enough to buy drinks by the company he kept. Justine giggled in amusement but let her face became serious as she started speaking again.

"Twenty one years ago tomorrow we found you in the street, alone and helpless. I've cared for you all of these years and look at you now," she stopped and waved her hand up and down, as if showing Casper off to an invisible crowd. "I just wish I knew where I went wrong." The grin on her face brightened the room as she jested. "Then I could've raised a true gentleman."

Justine began to laugh once again at her poorly thought out jokes. A kick to her shin from Casper's foot made her laugh even louder. Knowing she was embarrassing Casper with her laughter made it all the more funny. A few more kicks from Casper quieted her down and she slowly regained control of her breathing. Casper started to speak, only to be interrupted by Noel, who dropped a plate of food that Casper could only begin to guess what it was meant to be.

"All alone tonight?" he asked, turning his head to speak directly to the masculine Neanderthal hulking above him.

"Yup," Noel replied hoarsely. "My little Casey took the night off for a party with her friends."

Casey was Noel's pride and joy. Now twenty two, Noel had raised her in the bar since she could walk and talk and was taking orders soon afterwards. Having lost his wife when she gave birth to their daughter, Casey was all he had. It was a strain providing all of her needs, but he found ways to do it. He would do anything for his little princess.

Considering she was being raised in a bar, Casper often wondered why the owners had never objected to this form of child rearing. These thoughts only led him to question if Beezel's even had owners or if time had just made everyone forget who owned the unsanitary hell hole that had congealed into a bar. He looked back up to find Noel still looking down at him.

"You about Casey's age, right?" he said squinting. Casper just nodded his head in response. "Good, she could use a man like you." He laughed, slapping Casper on his back before departing. Casper winced slightly in response to the rough contact. Turning back to the new plate before them, he studied it in hopes to learn its secret identity. Sighing in exasperation, he looked to Justine for an answer.

"Chili dogs," She responded to his questioning stare.

"Could've fooled me." Sliding one of the dogs off the plate and into his hand, he could feel the sickening food squish in his fist. The chili dog left a slimy residue in his hand as he forced it into his mouth. Shaking his hand vigorously, he learned that the residue was too resistant to be shaken off so settled for scraping it off on the side of the table.

Justine sat in her seat, looking at Casper with a somber look upon her face as if she were weighing heavy thoughts. Casper, oblivious to her gaze, continued eating and only stopped when Justine finally spoke.

"I need a new job," She sighed. "I can't go back to the warehouse. Not where Ben works. Anywhere but there." Casper tried to reply but failed to create comprehendible words with the bar's sickly concoctions in his mouth, so chewed a few times and swallowed so as to respond quickly.

"Come to work with me on Monday, I'll be in the shop and I'm sure Jesse could use a few new cashiers in there." The antique store Jesse owned had only two real cashiers who constantly needed time off and Jesse was in desperate need of a new, more reliable worker. He was not particularly fond of using his movers as shopkeepers and only used them if he had no other choice.

Justine grinned at his offer. It was exactly what she was hoping to hear from him. She reached over and grabbed a chili dog off the plate and started to take a bite until she realized that Casper was rubbing his neck. The burns he had received earlier from the mysterious white flash still stung Casper and he was subconsciously aware of it. Leaning in, Justine studied his neck. Seeing the burned streak across his neck made her gasp slightly and lean in closer.

"What happened to you?" she asked riddled with concern. Raising her hand so it almost touched the burn, she held it there, taking extra care not to touch the skin. Casper instinctively pulled back away from the hand and covered his neck up to conceal the burns.

"Nothing, I'll be fine," he said. "Just a little wound from work." Justine squinted, trying to get a better look through his hand. She knew he was lying, as there would be nothing to burn his neck on at work, at least not like that. Leaning even closer, she propped both her hands on the unclean table to push herself forward for a better view. In response to this, he pushed himself backwards to escape her gaze, leaning once again onto the two back legs. As they leaned, almost in unison, Casper lost his balance point on the chair. The sound of him hitting the unclean floor resounded throughout the bar, making the ambient noises die out almost immediately. The entire bar looked on as he picked himself up off the floor and brushed his clothes off before returning his seat to its upright position.

The crowd grumbled angrily and returned to their previous conversations as Casper sat back down, pretending nothing had just happened. The bar was full of unruly scoundrels who would jump at a chance to start a brawl in the building. Knowing this, he tried to avoid a fight by ignoring everyone until the bar resumed its naturally noisy state. One table however, did not lose interest on Casper. Uproarious laughter from the table made Casper and Justine look over towards the noise. Sitting only a few tables away, Casper saw a familiar face and being noticed made him laugh even harder. It was the banker that had taken the elderly woman's house the day before. Surrounded by three younger girls, Casper knew the guy was having his own private party. The banker stood up and stumbled the short distance between the tables to confront Casper.

"Heyyyyyy...hey I know you..." he stuttered. "You're that stupid little kid who thinks he's all important!" Casper shrunk away from the banker's foul breath as alcohol filled the air around him. "Hey..." He started again. "I've got one...two....uh...three...girls," he murmured, counting the girls at his table as he spoke. The three girls giggled as he pointed them out. "And you...you've got...one?" he asked as he turned to Justine, who looked back with a disgusted look on her face. "Looks like I...I'm the better man." Pointing to himself, he let out a slight belch.

"Those girls are young enough to be your daughters," Casper spat back.

"Oh, what's wrong, jealous?" The banker asked in fake sympathy, then turned towards Justine. "Hey sweetheart why don't you ditch this loser and come hang out with us." Leaning close to Justine's face, she could smell the disgusting stench of alcohol and cigarettes. "But first a...kiss." He added, closing his eyes and puckering his lips. He drew his face close to Justine's as she backed away from him. Looking down into her hand, she realized the chili dog still lay in her possession, untouched. Smiling wickedly, Justine pushed the food into the banker's lips and smashed it into his face. A roar could be heard emanating from his mouth throughout the entire bar, muffled by the chili dog as he spit out chunks of food.

"Here, wash it down with this!" Justine squealed in delight, all too proud of herself, as she tossed the contents of her beer bottle into the angry man's face. The cheap beer made him yell even louder as he wiped the drink from his eyes. Taking a step back, he lost his balance, too drunk to stay upright. Still laughing, Justine took her eyes off of the moaning man to scan the room. She noticed that her actions had once again gotten the bar room's attention and everyone was waiting for the anticipated fight.

She jumped atop their table with amazing agility and motioned towards herself as she yelled "whose next?" Everyone grumbled, even angrier this time. If there were any rules to follow at Beezel's, the most important was to treat women with respect and not land a blow on one. Anyone caught harming Justine would instantly become the public enemy and would have to answer the entire bar room. All the men began to grin when Noel looked up to question Justine.

"Is this guy bothering you? Want us to take care of him?" he asked, pointing from the bar to the mumbling banker.

"No, its fine, I think he learned his lesson." She answered, getting down from her perch. "Sorry about your table." She added without stopping to think about how pointless the apology was.

"Hey it's alright, maybe you're shoes took some of that trash off of it," he said, turning back to his duties at the bar.

The room once again resumed their private affairs as she grimaced at the thought of what was on the table may now be on her shoes.

Casper had laughed at the whole situation but realized that Justine would soon remember the strange burn marks on his neck. He preferred it if people wouldn't worry and doctor him. After all, he could take care of himself.

"I need to get some fresh air," he stated, standing abruptly. "I'll be right back in. Order yourself some more beer." With a flick, he tossed some of the stolen cash on the table. Before she could object, he forced his way over to the door and made his way outside, stopping only a moment to look and ensure that Justine was not following him. She had taken his advice and gone to the bar for another beer. The banker meanwhile, was back up on his feet, stumbling clumsily in the direction of Casper.

"I'll get you, just you wait!" He yelled dizzily across the room, "What's wrong, too…too afraid to fight?" he asked with each step. Casper grinned at the drunk's weak threats before turning back toward the door. The sounds of the dogs on the hunt sounded much closer Casper noticed as the door swung open and the hinges squeaked in protest.

Exiting the building, he walked a few steps into the cool night air before hearing the dog's again. Only then did he realize why the dog's barking and howling were much clearer and closer, as if they were in the town. As he turned around, his heart stuttered and skipped beats while fear ate away at him.

Chapter 6

Even though Casper assumed what he saw was a trick of the dim street lights, he was still filled with a terror that rooted him to the spot. A pack of six dogs stood ready to fight, impatiently waiting for the command from the men and women standing around them. The humans looked at Casper, grinning maliciously while stroking the beasts standing next to them. Unable to recognize the breed of dogs, Casper wondered if any human could accurately guess their origin. The six of them ranged only slightly in size. The smallest was the size of a lion and the leader of the pack as big as a race horse.

Nausea ripped Casper's stomach apart at the sight of the monsters. He couldn't begin to contrive where exactly these creatures could have come from, but could only surmise one answer. They must be a breed unknown to Earth, as if Hell's own fiery pits had bred them. Red in color with black accents strewn throughout their body, he instantly knew these dogs were meant for killing and started to feel as if he was the prey they had been seeking this whole time. The scent of their hides reached his nostrils and the scent of a thousand dead men made Casper audibly sick, almost relieving his stomach of its contents as he gagged. This made the men and women next to the beasts snicker in unison, as if it were a private joke.

Regaining his breath, he looked up slowly in hopes that his horrors had disappeared but found the creatures staring him down. Saliva, dark and thick as blood oozed out of their mouths through the gaps as their fangs were shown while they bared their teeth in devilish growls. An unfortunate soul trapped in fear, Casper felt the world around him turning darker as if pure evil was taking over and claiming all the earthly land and turning it alien. A bark shot out of one of the hound's snouts, spraying shining projectiles of saliva and rotten debris into a grimy mist, making Casper jump. Terror drew tight as Casper prepared to run. Mentally choosing a path to avoid death, he tensed his right foot in an attempt to turn but before he got a chance, the sound of a slamming door distracted every creature on the street. Looking back towards Beezel's, everyone saw that the drunken banker had finally made his way to the door and now staggered clumsily into the street. He caught sight of Casper and smiled as a drunk would.

"Ha, you ready to fight then are you?" He asked, pointing to Casper while trying to keep his balance. "Look at the….look at your face. You're terrified…to… to uh…fight me." He announced proudly. "Well…you…"

The drunk was cut off sharply by the creatures behind him. The largest dog snorted heavily on the banker's neck, catching his attention. His face lit up in terror as his eyelids opened widely. Stumbling to turn around, the banker finally noticed they were not alone in the street.

The unnaturally large dog lowered his head to meet the banker's face and seemed to smile devilishly while still quivering its upper lip to let the blood-like drool slide off his fangs. The sight could make even Satan's blood run cold. Looking past the banker, Casper realized that the humans no longer stood with the dogs, but in there stead were wolves, viciously staying with the dogs and adding to their overall awesome presence. The banker's head rolled in drunken horror to take in the sight as he gurgled within his throat, not knowing what to do. A high pitched screech finally came forth from his lips, shaking everyone and shattering the tension much like a rock hitting a mirror. Casper took this as a cue to run and spun in the opposite direction. Using his muscular legs, he fled as fast as he could from the bar.

Casper winced at the sounds the banker made somewhere behind as he screamed and gasped for breath. Being sprayed by blood, Casper sneaked a painful look behind him and dread forced his head back around. The creatures had only been minutely inconvenienced by the banker and were just a few short steps behind him. Blood rained down from above as the largest beast ran with the banker's body locked tight in his jowls. Not even bothering to even kill the drunk in mercy, he chased Casper with the man still living. Casper heard the man screaming for help as he was thrashed viciously about in the monster's hold. Even though he tried his best to block out the horrifying sounds behind him, the air was permeated with the horrid shouts as he continued running down the street.

Scanning the town around him, Casper searched desperately for a way to escape the encroaching monstrosities just a few feet away. Running to the right, he frantically leapt onto a porch and ran a few steps across the outside wall to bank his velocity. Hitting the porch floor while still in motion, he reached the other end where a railing was standing in his path. Reaching both hands in front of him, he grabbed the railing firmly and vaulted on top of it, where he perched himself precariously. In one fluid motion, his leg muscles launched his body off into the dark night, allowing him to grab a window sill jutting from the second story of the neighboring house. He felt the creature's bloody nose as his legs nicked the dog's face. The dogs had reached him and he whimpered slightly as they leapt up from the ground, trying to grab a chunk of his flesh.

Grasping the wooden sill desperately, he pulled his body up and through the open window, letting his body drop inside a bedroom. Before even catching his breath, he rolled to his feet and sighed in a short lived relief. The sound of a door being knocked in downstairs made him realized that he was far from safe. Like a stampede, he heard the hounds destroying the first floor in search of a means to reach him. If it weren't for the fact that his life was in danger, he would have laughed at the idea that they were destroying the stairs in the process. Instead, terror forced him to run towards a closed door, which he pushed open and rushed into a bathroom where a lady had just been enjoying a relaxing bath before the sounds of monsters downstairs tore her out of relaxation. She screamed at Casper, who in return, kept his eyes focused on the window across the room.

"Hope you have house insurance!" He yelled just before leaping through the closed window. Shattering glass followed him outside and rained onto the wall of a nearby house as he landed on it. Using his feet as brakes, he slid down the wall to fall safely on the ground. "Just wait till they find out I'm not up there," he grinned.

Joy melted in alarm. The hellish beasts made their own doorway through the side of the house and into the alleyway, fresh on his scent. A gruesome sound could be heard as the banker's neck snapped. Long past dead, the largest barbaric dog bashed a hole large enough for him to pass through but in doing so, detached the head from the body, making it airborne until a nearby hound lunged and caught it. Wincing, Casper watched as it gripped the head it in its powerful jaws and heard the man's skull crush as it snapped its jaws close.

Casper became aware that these dogs were not a trick of light and his life was in more danger than ever. He wished Ben had killed him earlier. At least then he would be bestowed with mercy and not a monster's meal. The dogs slowly formed a line between the two houses. As they crept forward, Casper wondered why they didn't just attack and just gazed back at him with their evil smile. An attempt to retreat quickly answered his question. The maniacal wolves had formed a matching line on the other side of him and blocked any chance of escape. Looking back and forth in desperation, he looked for any way to get away from the deadly jaws of doom.

All the animals seemed to be pleased with their little trap and slowly moved in to kill the overly frightened man. With no where to turn Casper awaited death, while his subconscious mind sought any way to save himself from the ill fate about to unfold.

An idea shocked Casper back into reality and an adrenaline rush cleared his mind so he could focus. He had one shot to escape the dark alley and could not afford to mess up. Facing the wolves, he crouched in a running position, making the wolves stare on in curiosity. With a push off, he ran the short distance between himself and the animals, but just as he reached their line he jumped sideways and planted himself to the wall. His legs absorbed energy from the jump as he squat his body against the wall. Pushing off with the will to live, he spun, letting his body dive towards the line and at the same releasing, his knife from his jeans. Unleashing a hellish attack from above, Casper slashed at the closest wolf during mid dive. As the blade drew a wicked scar across its back, it whined and shrank away, letting Casper sail through the newly created gap in the line. He landed in a roll that brought him to his feet. Without a pause, Casper launched back into a terrified run with all the strength he could muster as the pack regrouped and started back in on the chase. With alarm he looked down toward his hand to where the knife was firmly gripped. The wolfen blood on the blade sizzled as if it had caught fire when it exited the wolf's wound, but no flames appeared. Grimacing, he looked forward for a new plan of action. The animals were determined to drink his blood and evidently smart enough to not be outwitted by the likes of him.

Twin beams of light turned from a corner to land squarely on his chest. Like piercing yellow eyes, he confused them for another nightmare wanting to feed on his living flesh and slowed only slightly to reevaluate his situation. As his eyes processed the information before him, a truck took shape in his vision. With desperation, he ran blindly at the oncoming vehicle, quickly closing the gap between himself and the truck. The driver, who had not seen Casper, suddenly became aware of the hideous dog like things about to collide with his truck. With terror across his face, he pushed his brakes instantly to the floor. Casper heard the squealing tires and could smell burning rubber, but didn't serve to slow him down on his mad dash.

Gathering any speed he could, he reached the truck at full speed with the pack of beasts near his heels. Using the momentum as an advantage, he sprung off the ground and landed with his left foot on the truck's hood. Without losing a second, he pushed off the trucks hood, leaving only a dent as he planted both feet onto the roof of the stopped truck. Every part of Casper drove him forward in hopes of escape as he jumped off the roof to roll in the bed of the truck. His dive was jolted when the hideous monsters, which apparently had not had the distance to stop, collided with the truck, forcing it backwards. The sound of metal crunching and demonic growling forced him to stop his roll and scramble up to a standing position. His movement continued forward as he flipped front wards out of the truck bed and landed on the ground, bending his knees to absorb the blow. Casper never knew just how agile he was, but fear of death made his muscles know how to move acrobatically without practice. As his legs hit the ground, he heard a mighty explosion behind him engulfing the truck. Looking back to the side walk, he saw the former truck driver standing in anger, screaming at the sight. Heat washed over his face as Casper was forced to throw his hands up in protection while he tried to look back to where the truck was now in flames. The smoke cleared away from the scene as a strong breeze blew by, revealing something he was not prepared for. One dog, which he could only guess to be the one who took the brunt of the truck's blow, now crawled over the car, crushing the cab with each paw as he stepped. The other dogs, followed closely by the wolves in the pack, stalked out around the flaming truck, simpering with pride.

Casper took no time as he ran once again from the abominations. Realizing that the pack was closing in on him made his muscles bulge as he ran even harder in attempts to push himself further ahead of the ghoulish beasts. His run could not save him entirely and he felt the ghastly hot breath of a nearby dog on his calves as they ran with ease. It took a minute for Casper to remember that his knife was still gripped tightly in his hand, but once realization struck he swung it blindly behind his body to where he could feel the breath originate from. A yelping sound reassured Casper that his swing had found its mark and caused the dog to back down slightly. Not quick enough for a second strike, a dog caught up with him on his other side and threw a paw out, catching his leg and scraping the skin.

Casper yelled in pain but couldn't afford to slow down lest the monsters catch him. Switching the blade between his hands, he swung quickly to slice the attacker's nose. Hearing a growl, he knew the blade barely hit its skin but caused it pain nonetheless.

Blood welled up from the fresh wound and ran down along his leg as he tried to ignore the horrendous pain. Although only a minor laceration, it felt as if the beast had ripped his leg wide open and lit his tendons on fire. He needed to stop and rest soon. The cuts on the back of his leg were already making him limp and he could feel his energy draining away from his body. No longer able to recognize the surrounding houses, he wondered what part of town he had stumbled into. The only thing he knew at this point was that he was surely not in a place he had ever visited and therefore would no longer know of a place to escape their wrath. As if by magic, a moon beam cut through the clouds above and landed on a building directly in front of him. The road ended in a three way intersection and his only means of safety appeared to be in the building. A sturdy wooden doorway arched in the middle of the building's façade, bearing two doors that met in the arch's center. Barely convinced that these doors could keep his pursuers away, he at least hoped he could lose them inside. Sprinting with any shred of energy he could surmise, he made a run for the door.

Feet pounding and heart pumping, Casper reached the stone steps with inhuman speed and climbed the short distance to the top where the doors awaited him. With a great heave, one door opened from his push and began sliding inside. An angry growl echoed in the streets, causing him to turn around in surprise. The dogs had stopped short of the giant stone steps, but the wolves showed no signs of slowing as they raced down with determination toward the door. With a foolish hope of survival, Casper flung his precious knife into the street. Sinking deeply in flesh, the blade nestled itself into one of the figures, causing it to let out an unearthly screech that made Casper instantly hope he would never hear again. As to which one it had hit, he was not sure.

A wolf had run ahead of the others, now leaping up the steps, he was now on a collision course with Casper's sweating face. Blood pumping from adrenaline, he slammed the mighty door closed and chuckled when he heard the thud of the wolf's body as it slammed head first into the wooden barrier.

Yet another wolfen cry was let out, making him shudder at its blood curdling sound.

Sighing in great relief, Casper realized that the creatures were not following him into the building. Looking through a small stained glass window, he could barely make out the visages of evil lining up on the street, waiting impatiently for him to walk out the building but seemingly too afraid to venture close. He turned around and started limping towards the inner sanctions of whatever building he was now prisoner of. While clutching his injured leg, he looked around the tall building. Fatigue and post adrenaline effects made it impossible for him to rationalize where he was. Giving up in exhaustion, Casper limped to one of the many benches littering the structure's main room. Falling onto the bench, the sweet call of sleep closed his eyes and carried him to a safe haven of dreams. In his trance, he was oblivious to the man staring at him from the other side of the room.

Chapter 7

"Why must our dreams dance our hearts to sleep?" Casper heard a deep voice as it resonated throughout the mighty building, awakening him from his sleep. Unsure of the time, he could at least tell that some hours had passed since his run through the streets of Heresen. Opening one eye, he scratched his head while looking around, still feeling overly tired.

The stained glass windows around him let in light from the moon and the colored light danced lazily on the stone surfaces in the room as clouds passed across the lunar sphere. The building's interior let Casper figure out where he had stumbled into. A podium and alter stood proudly in front of a giant wooden cross. A Christian church surrounded him, making the room's surroundings feel instantly uncomfortable.

"Come forth my child and seek redemption." The strange voice called, beckoning him forward. Looking for the source, he assumed the man speaking was sitting inside the confessional, which consisted of two small wooden cubes separated by an intricately carved wall. Pain drew Casper back to his leg. A short burst of pain forced him to look down, but as he examined the wounds on his leg he saw any damage done by the dog had healed over. Only the burning feeling remained, which felt a lot like the burns he received on his neck. He rubbed his calf in attempts to soothe the burn but only succeeded in worsening the pain. Giving up in a sigh, he got up and started walking slowly to the door, limping slightly on the way. Rain started to splatter against the roof, sounding off reverberations throughout the empty church and comforting the limping man. If anything were to make him feel better, it'd be a walk in the rain. Maybe it would even wake him from the horrendous nightmare that had encompassed his life.

"I wouldn't go out there, it's dangerous," warned the mystifying voice as Casper reached for the door. Looking backward, he peered through the darkness to find its owner. The moon had been covered by the rain clouds and vision was limited to a few lit candles strewn throughout the sanctuary. Realizing that he would not be able to find the talking man hiding in the confessional, he gave up with a sigh.

"I think I can handle a little bit of rain!" the perturbed man yelled back as he turned back to the door. Pulling on its giant handle, he freed the ancient door from its home in the doorway. He squeezed outside, glad to feel the refreshing rain collect on his skin. The door stayed open as he walked down the stone steps. A dim street light flickered close by and Casper suddenly lost interest in the rain. Outlined by the erratic lighting was a jaw line punctuated by fangs and wet with red ooze. It suddenly occurred to Casper that one of the dogs was sitting at the bottom of the stairs, waiting patiently for him to come out. A flash of lighting sent light throughout the city. In its brilliance, he could make out the shapes of the rest of the pack of monsters waiting to feast on his entrails. This gave him enough encouragement to forget his hurt leg and jump back up the steps. With a dive, he rolled through the open doorway. Landing on his stomach, he skidded onto his back and slammed the door shut with a kick. Standing up slowly, the shaken man brushed the rain off his shoulders.

"I wasn't talking about the rain," The distant voice answered in response to the slamming door. "They'll be out there all night and will only leave with the sunrise." Casper shot a venomous glance into the dark church. He was getting tired of the world's recent mysteries. It would seem that this would be his safe haven for the time being, so he would make the best of it.

"What the hell are those things? They almost killed me and wrecked half the town!" He slowly walked towards the voice, no longer bothered by his injuries.

"Those were a concoction of the devil himself," was his only response as Casper's shoes slapped against the worn tiles.

"Yeah I figured you'd say that. Everything you people don't agree with must be the devil in disguise, right?" Enraged at the obvious response to his question, Casper yelled blindly towards the confessional.

The voice replied in its calm tone. "You don't understand. Those were hell hounds. Beasts bred in Satan's own breeding grounds. They won't stop until you're dead." This made Casper pause. He didn't believe in religion but it was the only explanation to the danger lurking outside. Clearing his throat, he thought deeply about his answer before speaking again.

"And the wolves, what are they then, the devil's lapdogs?" A heavy sigh haunted the church just before an explanation was started.

"Those were therions, only partially wolf. They're human's who've sold their souls to the devil for immortality." Casper pondered long on this response.

"So they're..." he stopped, cringing at how stupid he was about to sound, "werewolves then?" finishing the sentence with great sarcasm. He could hear the voice growling with impatience at Casper's apparently simple questions.

"No, werewolves are creatures of story and legend. Having no control of their powers or instincts, they are nothing more than a cover up of the truth. Therions, on the other hand, are capable of shape shifting at will. They also have command over the hell hounds. They are their keepers, masters if you will."

The strange words surrounded Casper as he walked slowly towards the confessional. Hard as it was to believe in what happened to him over the course of the last couple of days, it was even harder for him to believe what he was now hearing.

"How do you know these things?" He queried, slowing his steps. "Who are you?" Silence befell the church, and the softening echoes of his voice made him feel uneasy.

"I am blessed by this church so that I know about the beasts of Hell. While in this church you are safe. They cannot cross the threshold as ordered by the powers of GOD." This answer pierced the silence and filled the room once again with the knowledgeable voice. Listening closely, Casper knew he had heard the voice somewhere before but could not place who it belonged to. He glanced around the room, taking in all the details that it held as he thought of the sanctuary's powers of protection.

"Come, sit by me. You seem troubled and I believe I can settle your mind with conversation." Snapping his gaze back to the front, he glared at the confessional. With a moment's pause, he gave in with a sigh and crossed the room to where the confessional's empty bench stood and sat in the uncomfortable seat to look through the wall at the figure on the other side. He could barely make out facial features of the man on the other side of the wall with which he had been speaking with. Staring back at each for only a moment, both men sat in serenity.

"So as long as I'm in here I'm safe. No one can hurt me?" Casper asked, trying to get a better look through the wooden structure between them. "Your God will protect me?"

The man lowered his head into his hands. "It's more complicated then that," he said in exasperation. "He is not my God. He is GOD and he does not exist to serve you…" At this point the man paused. Choosing wise words, he continued the lecture. "There is an ongoing battle between Heaven and Hell that everyone must one day learn about."

"Yes, we've all heard about your little war of good and evil. I'm not part of it, so I think I'll be fine without your little lecture." This caused the man to sit straight up in his chair. Obviously something Casper said had caught his attention. He could feel the man's anger wafting from the booth next to him.

"You have no idea what this war means to you." He said to him through gritted teeth, "but war is in your blood. One way or another it will end your life."

"What the hell are you talking about? What does the eternal forces of your God need of an orphan like me? Just leave me alone!" He shouted while slamming his fists against the confessional, causing the figure on the other side to lift his head out of cupped hands and face him. Black eyes glared back at him with an unknown rage.

"Your wrists are cut with the mark of a cyspherion. You are no ordinary orphan, Michael." This response, accompanied by the glaring black eyes made Casper quiver slightly in fear. Shocked that he had known about the markings, he could only gasp a response. He pulled his hands back quickly out of reflex and gripped them against his chest.

"What the hell is a cyspherion?" He screamed, tears streaming down his face. Painful thoughts of his life and the tattoos surfaced. Everyone seemed to know about his past except for him. Unable to control himself, he wept bitterly for the stranger. "God Damn it who are you and how do you know me?" These questions shook the church and settled to an eerie silence. The sobbing slowed down as he eventually regained control of himself. "Who are you?" he asked in a quiet tone.

Lightening streaked across the sky, illuminating the church and highlighting the face behind the wooden wall. He instantly recognized the features outlined by long white hair. Shock ran through him as the song of metal could be heard as it was released from its sheath.

"Wyburn," He muttered in shock, just barely able to vocalize the name before metal came crashing through the intricate wall. Wood splintered all around him as a sword blade came destructively through the confessional. A katana came to rest on his neck, threatening his very existence.

"Yes, it's me," Wyburn answered, leaning forward. "And I believe you have something of mine." he pushed the blade forward as Casper tried to back away from its deadly sheen. Sweat dripped from his skin onto the weapon, making it refract the dim candlelight. Casper could feel the cold steel against his skin, almost cutting and killing him. Letting out a small whimper, terror anchored him to the bench, almost too afraid to even move. With shaking nerves, he slid his hands quickly into his pockets to frantically search for the little cloth pouch. Trepidation scorched his soul as he pulled the object free of the jean pocket. Arms quivering, he dangled it through the hole in the divider towards Wyburn while still cowering from the blade. An instant reaction arose from Wyburn. Lowering his sword he instantly snatched the sack from Casper and held it as if it were dear to him. Fear slowly lifted and Casper began to stare in bewilderment at Wyburn's actions. Sensing the man looking up at him Wyburn stuffed the pouch into a hidden pocket within his coat.

"It's my wife's," he explained quickly looking back up. Casper still couldn't clear the confusion in his mind. Pushing himself off the seat, he stood up and walked quickly out of the tiny booth.

"It's just a ball of cheap metal," he finally replied while brushing himself off. This made Wyburn's eyes center on his unprotected back. The katana was firmly returned to its sheath before he rose to his feet.

"So you opened it? You looked inside?" he asked, slowly putting his hands onto Casper's shoulders, making him feel uneasy. "You touched my only possession?" Casper turned his head to the side in an attempt to try and see Wyburn better.

"Yeah, it's pretty useless. I wouldn't even get five pieces for it," he replied snidely, no longer thinking about the sword resting at Wyburn's side. Wyburn drew back and gave a swift backhand to Casper's head. "Ouch! What the hell? What did you expect…?" he started while clutching his head where he had been struck.

"It's not cheap metal," Wyburn snapped, eyes burning. "It's not even a type of metal." Mutual animosity sparked around the two as they stared back at each other.

"Oh yeah, then what is it, some stupid marriage ball?" He sneered back. Wyburn took a step back and looked downwards. Casper's words had cut through Wyburn's heart like a knife and he could tell his words had deeply affected him in some way. He almost felt bad for the old man as it was no place for him to be insulting Wyburn for something when he himself had just stolen something of value from him.

"Its angel's blood," he said finally with a slight sniffle, looking back up. "When an angel dies, they can be summoned by the powers of their blood." Casper stared at the old man. Perhaps the obviously insane old man had escaped the

Faulkland Asylum, he thought in his mind. Wyburn looked back to meet his reserved look. Dismissing Casper's obvious thoughts of his sanity, Wyburn continued his explanation.

"This blood," he said, pulling the bag back out of his pocket, "was the blood of my wife, Aspriel. She fell in battle just after you were born." Tears came to Wyburn's eyes, summoned by the past he had tried to forget. Casper continued to contemplate the man's mental status, but the name Aspriel had made him jump. Memories of the woman in the mirror came back to him in an instant.

"Maybe you're not as crazy as you sound." Casper said in awe. "That…stuff, the angel blood, it melted on my hand. It said Aspriel, and then this girl appeared in a mirror…" he trailed off in thought. "But wait," he picked up again, "Why did it only work for me. Justi…" he paused. "My friend touched it and nothing happened. She said it was just a ball of pewter."

"So you talked to her?" Wyburn asked, turning slowly. "The powers of angel blood can only be unlocked by those with superior blood lines." Casper looked at him in complete confusion.

"Why the hell would I have a superior bloodline? What the hell are you talking about?" He asked.

"A superior bloodline comes from the born followers of the two alignments," answered the now pacing Wyburn. "We are conceived of angels. Our nemesis leads the hordes of demons." He paused and looked over to Casper, giving him full attention. "Aspriel, the girl you talked to…" he said slowly, "is your mother."Wyburn's words filled Casper with a strange feeling he had never experienced before. He might just find out who his real parents were for the first time in his life. Snapping back into reality, he looked to where Wyburn now stood with his back to him.

"But that would mean…" the young man stuttered. "that would make you…father?" he finally asked. Wyburn turned and he could just barely make out the anger on his face before a bolt of light came streaking from his raised palm, striking Casper squarely in the chest. The smell of burnt skin billowed from his chest as he was knocked back by the blow. Hitting the door with his back, Casper was held up against it by the continuing beam. The sound of impact had agitated the hell hounds and they barked and howled in excitement and fury in hopes that a tasty meal would be thrown out of the church so they could rend him asunder. He could only groan as the blast of light held him in place.

"You're a bastard child!" Casper could hear Wyburn yelling as his voice combated the crackling of the lightening bolt. "You have no father!" The silhouette of the old man walking slowly towards him, palm still raised made him shudder. Flailing with all the strength left in his body, he attempted unsuccessfully to break the lightning's grip on him.

"Hey, stop it!" he gasped in failure. "You're burning me!" Wyburn lowered his palm in response as the air about him seemed to lose a little of the anger. "I'm not a child," he said in disdain, falling to the floor. Finally released from the painful light, he could feel his usual cocky nature returning. "I'm almost twenty one." He groaned as he rubbed his chest to soothe the burn.

"Foolish boy," Anger flared as Wyburn's eyes were consumed by their own blackness. "I am two hundred and forty three years old. I was fighting wars long before you were even created!"

"Hey, cool down," Casper back lashed, "It's not my fault your wife slept around." He soon learned that this was a mistake. The air around Wyburn quivered as if they were consumed in flames as he seemed to grow in size. The dark holes that made up his eyes started to glow in their deep black color. The hellish radiation of air was being generated from his back. Without warning, two gigantic wings shot out from either side of Wyburn. The impressive wingspan was made of luminously white feathers and spread a staggering fifteen feet. This sudden change in appearance made Casper cover his body in feeble protection, terrified of the creature before him.

"Don't you ever dare even insinuate that Aspriel could love another!" Though Casper could hear the sound of Wyburn's voice, it was as if he was talking in his head, reverberating through his mind and causing his head to hurt. "You were a mistake. You should never have been created!" Looking up, he noticed the angel's lips were no longer moving. Moving his hands away from his face, Casper could only stare upwards in awe at the looming creature. "Your mother is dead." He continued. "Show her whatever shred of dignity you have left. She was a hundred times the angel you will ever be!"

Completing his speech, he calmed down and the angry cloud of energy started to dissipate. Moments passed, stretching the silence to an infinite pain. Casper dared not speak. Still awestruck, he decided it best to not make Wyburn any angrier than he had just been. Looking back at the figure made him gasp. Wyburn's wrists bore the same cross that was tattooed on his wrist as well as the one that appeared in the angelic blood. The only notable differences were that Wyburn's name was written within the cross and there was nothing bordering his cross. In the shallow breaths escaping Casper's lungs, he murmured illogical words, unable take his gaze off the marked wrists. This sudden interest made Wyburn look down.

"I think there is a lot you have yet to learn," he said, sliding his hand across the marked wrists. "You need to realize who you truly are." Casper, slightly irritated at this response watched Wyburn as he folded his wings down against his back, taking away from his awesome appearance.

"How am I suppose to learn anything when everyone seems to know more about me then I do?" He asked, feeling a little safer without the giant wings in front of him. "No one wants to tell me what's happening. How the hell should I know what a cyspherion is?

"Easy," was the response that rolled out of Wyburn's smile. "I'll show you." Before Casper could object, Wyburn's deadly palm came up and he held it just inches from Casper's face. "Just relax," he cooed just as he slammed his open hand against Casper's face. A blinding flash exploded all around him. Though it did not burn him this time, Casper was equally terrified about what was happening. The flash made him lose consciousness. His eyes rolled to the back of his head and ecstasy took over his brain.

Chapter 8

GOD created all that there is. He is the infallible being with ultimate control. Being the balance of light and dark, He realized that the powers of good and evil must be kept in check. For one could not exist without the other. When done creating earth, He created two Sages. These brother Sages, named Zeus and Cronus, were to rule the world and ensure GOD'S will be done to keep a perfect balance. Zeus was the sage of honor while his brother, Cronus, was the sage of malice.

Casper regained consciousness to find himself in an eternal void. Suspended in pure darkness, he heard whispers throughout his head. As he listened, he slowly learned the true war of good and evil.

Being opposite in nature, the two brothers were constantly fighting each other. Unable to get along, but impossible for one to live without the other, turmoil swept the land. What GOD had dread the most had come to pass. In a final fight held within their throne room, Zeus threw Cronus from their domain to a treacherous prison called Tartarus. Proud of his uncouth act, Zeus sent a messenger to earth to boast. The legendary Hercules was born. By order of Zeus, Hercules was instructed to tell humans that the evil Cronus was dethroned and to praise the mighty God Zeus. When GOD returned to inspect how his sages had been handling their jobs, Zeus tried to deny the truth and told GOD that Cronus had dejected from his post and was hiding in shame.

Lights began to dance around Casper, responding to each word spoken in his head. Looking on in amazement he could do nothing but float and listen to the tales of ancient religion spun around him. The mysterious aura about him made it seem all too real.

There was no fooling the omnipotent GOD. Enraged by Zeus' actions, He took immediate action. In thunderous words He told the sages that they had done their jobs poorly and their immortality was being revoked. The once proud sages became battle mages locked into an eternally forsaken war. Tartarus was transformed into the pits of Hell where Cronus ruled. He eventually took on the name Satan to help employ followers on Earth as Cronus was hated from the lies of Hercules. GOD then sent his own son to earth to repair what had gone wrong. Christianity was born from the savior Jesus as he taught people who GOD was and told them to praise his holiness. The teachings were lost on human's limited ability to comprehend a perfect being. One such as GOD should not be flawed with such that he is solely good, for it would be an imperfection. Instead, He controlled good and evil alike as they were both created by him, making him above everyone and everything else. The humans, however, began preaching that God and Satan were locked on equal planes of power of good and evil. Though GOD was above all things including good and evil, he was reduced merely to what Zeus had once been. In return the world greatly suffered as GOD unleashed his wrath upon those who could not understand GOD's true powers. Without Zeus' knowledge, his followers murdered Jesus in false hopes of making him more powerful. The death was covered up by lies from the human race and Mythology took its course, letting everything came to pass as it was and not what it should be. Zeus and Satan continued their insatiable blood lust against each other. Heaven and Hell became safe havens for those who followed its leaders. GOD wept but planned for a day when wars would stop and his world would be at peace. Until then, the two battle mages will control armies against each other and each alignment will be branded by the wrists. Because Zeus' followers had recklessly killed Jesus, his forces are marked with crosses while Satan's powers are represented by a pentagram. Those with higher powers will be marked with a power symbol surrounding the symbol. The creature's name is determined by these markings as it is tattooed within its mark.

Fascinated by the stories, Casper let the words fall down around him until the last one echoed throughout the dark. Letting his eyes wander about, he soon realized they were still closed. Lifting his eyelids, a bright light filled his vision. As he focused, the world became less of a blur and he could start to see what was around him. He was suspended in midair as if held up by invisible wires inside an endless sea of white light. Looking around, he found that Wyburn was next to him, also held up by the invisible force. Close by was a shrouded floating figure. He looked at the creature curiously, unable to ascertain its mysteries or origin.

"It's a mystic lich," Wyburn said, scaring Casper out of his focus. "A manifestation of lost souls, they are capable of showing memories long forgotten by even the strongest minds. I've summoned H'izveral for you as it is one of the oldest of them and contains more memories than any other."

"So he's like what, an encyclopedia?" Casper asked, looking back towards Wyburn.

"Not a he, but rather an it. Created by the lost souls of men and women, it has no gender," he answered while looking knowledgably at Casper. "It is not an encyclopedia, but merely memories. It can only show you what it remembers from past times, but nothing else." He looked back at H'izveral who nodded in approval of the answer. They floated in silence for a moment before Casper spoke again.

"So all that he just told me is true?" He took his time asking Wyburn the question, who closed his eyes and mouthed a yes. "So what's it got to do with me?" Wyburn opened his eyes and looked towards the floating figure.

"Listen," he said pointing back at H'izveral. Without warning the space around them swirled around into a tornado. From nothingness came landscape Casper could recognize immediately. The three of them floated only feet above a plateau just outside the city limits of Heresen. It was a secluded spot often visited by him and his friends to hide from life's problems. The top was easily half a mile from one end to the other, stretching further than any other plateau around town. H'izveral raised its hand and the air shimmered. Two holes appeared on opposite sides of the plateau, as if it had torn space and time itself to reveal swirling vortexes. In one a bright light emitted while the other let out a darkly foreboding red light.

In the many holes between Heaven, Hell and Earth, the Wrokthien portals are the most powerful. Their close proximity is not coincidental, for this is the very place where GOD stripped Zeus and Cronus of their sage status. Both holes opened up simultaneously twenty one years ago for a monumental battle. It was believed that this would be the end of the war. Each leader sent its most powerful forces forward, leaving nothing in reserve.

As if on command, creatures began emerging from the portals dressed for battle. Casper could barely make out each side as they lined up in war formations. Studying the monsters about, he could recognize hellhounds, demons and therions among other bizarre forms from Hell's forces. From Heaven's gate came, among others, angels, griffons and lammasu. In the air swept giant colored dragon like beasts. A giant roar broke out from both sides and combined to a giant war cry. Two creatures stepped forward to lead the packs of creatures. A demon Casper safely assumed to be nine feet tall hailed from Hell, swinging a demonic battle axe before him. His shoulders were protected by spiked pads. The only other piece of clothing he wore was a loincloth attached around his waist. The leathery hide stuck to his skin was so tough, it would repel any attacker. His horns glinted with blood as he snorted, looking towards the opposing force.

Casper gazed over towards Heaven and gasped. Silhouetted by the other creatures was a solitary angel.

Although too far to see clearly, he instantly recognized the figure and knew the face. Aspriel stood at ready with a claymore grasp firmly in both of her hands. White armor clung firmly to her body almost like a second skin. The two leaders raised their weapons in the air causing the sides to silence their war cries. Tension built on the battlefield. Each creature stared on in quiet anticipation. Lightening streaked the sky, cutting the tension like a knife as the forces charged toward impending doom.

If this battle could decide the winner, then there were no taking chances in the war. The legions followed the two greatest warriors, Aspriel, an archangel and Dafierno the nether demon. Fearless and without emotion in battle, they would surely win the war. Fate would not be on either's side. Being the highest ranking generals on either side, the two creatures had never met until this battle.

The three of them watched in awe, anticipating the clash of fighting. As Aspriel ran towards Dafierno, sword drawn, she began to slow down as an angelic light started emitting around her. Determination lit across her face as she approached the mid point of battle. Dafierno raced onwards but stopped as he caught a glimpse of the light. Locked in the battle charge, Dafierno had lowered his head in a death rush but the sudden change had made him look up. Shock entered his face while he slowed to a sudden halt. Taking a step back while staring in wonder, the demon lowered his axe. He bent down to one knee and laid the weapon down in front of him and lowered his head in surrender, taking a knee before the charging angel.

Dafierno, being a nether demon, had never felt love. His only duty was to destroy and wreak havoc. The sudden sight of Aspriel's beautiful war form had thrown the monster off. For once in his life he thought of something other than bloodshed. Stuck in love's confusion, Dafierno surrendered to her. By the war laws of GOD, Aspriel was to take Dafierno as prisoner before the battle continued.

The spectators watched the next sequence, still in silence. The archangel stopped short of the beast on his knees. A slight look of surprise stole over her face but quickly turned to a somber, stone cold stare. As she held her claymore above her head in a victorious pose, the setting sun outlined her slender form. As the sword reached its climax, she started turning it to her right side. The sword caught the light as she swung it over her right shoulder and in the same fluid motion, lowered the point of the sword on her right side as the blade arced out in front of Aspriel. With muscles tensing, the angel let the blade fly towards Dafierno's unprotected neck. There was no protest from the demon as metal sliced through the leathery hide to rend the inner rotting flesh. A sickening gushing sound was heard throughout the battlefield when she forced the blade all of the way through his neck. With every ounce of strength in her body, Aspriel freed the claymore from Dafierno's neck as demonic gore clung to its shining metal, roaring in anger and hatred.

The sword sliced through the air, trailing black oozing blood and entrails of the neck behind it. The decapitated corpse crumbled to the ground, being freed of its head in such a barbaric manner. Dafierno's face showed a pathetic sight of hopeless love as it sailed through the air and smashed into the ground. Dirt and debris stuck to its fresh blood as it rolled away from the dying body, his features frozen forever in a look of longing.

Aspriel raised the blood soaked weapon over her head once again. Looking up at it, she smiled with accomplishment. Blood trickled down the blade and coated her quivering hands. Bloody rivulets ran down her strong arms while drops fell downward onto her head and pooled around her face. She glowed in an awesome brilliance as the entire plateau looked on in amazement at what had just occurred before them.

"What does this have to do with me?" asked the impatiently confused Casper. H'izveral only brought his hand to his face in a silence gesture then pointed back to where the body of Dafierno lay. Too distracted by Aspriel's victory pose, the armies had not seen what was occurring at her feet. As the blood flowed from the demon's neck, it congealed into a pool of black liquid. A strange wavering aura flowed ever so softly from the dead body to float just above the pooling liquid. Looking back at his mother, Casper realized her glowing body was letting off a small sliver of light. It quietly mixed with the cloud above the pool.

Legend tells of an incredible beast named cyspherion. Born of demon blood and conceived from feelings. An angel's hatred would mix with a demon's love to breathe life into the blood and give it shape. Half demon, half angel, its capabilities would be unmarked. Its creation could be GOD's last attempt to save earth from its impending doom. A counter balance of light and dark, the much weaker form of GOD would walk among mankind. Before then, it would need to reach maturity and let its powers manifest. It would first search for a worthy mother to take care of him.

The black ooze drew in the cloudy mixture above it and turned into a ball like shape. The congealed blood began to take a sickly formation. A sudden shout from behind her caught Aspriel's attention. Turning her heels in the dust, her sturdy foot bumped the anamorphous blob, causing it to roll across the plateau. As if having a mind of its own, the blob flew through the air and down towards Heresen.

"Aspriel!" a horrified younger Wyburn landed from flight behind her while shouting her name. Running in to close the distance between them, he stopped just next to her. "What have you done?" he asked with terror tearing his eyes wide open.

"I've slain Dafierno, Cronus' greatest soldier." She said triumphantly as she lowered the heavy claymore to her side.

"He was surrendering! You shouldn't have harmed him!" he yelled back.

A slow buzz radiated throughout the battlefield. Starting softly, it grew into a tremendous sound. Its earsplitting roar ripped the creatures' attention from Aspriel and back towards the two portals. Lightning netted itself across the holes, blocking any possible retreat.

Even in its creation, the cyspherion contained strong powers. Its unnatural presence conflicted with the powers of good and evil. Until his removal from the area, the powers locked within him would restrict travel through the Wrokthien portals. Forces from either side were charged with the task of finding and destroying the cyspherion.

The voice faded out as H'izveral turned its cloaked head towards Wyburn, who nodded. He raised his hand and the visions about them shimmered into darkness. Casper watched the lich fade away, taking its place once again among the darkness. The church emerged from around them until it completely replaced the shadows of memories. Moments ticked on like hours as Casper and Wyburn sat in silence.

"You are special and you can win this war once and for all." Wyburn said suddenly, making Casper look up in surprise.

"So what, I'm like some kind of wizard and now I have to go to some special academy and learn how to control my powers?" he asked, reverting to his usual cocky mannerism. Wyburn looked angrily back, glowering at the snide cyspherion.

"You foolish boy, this isn't a stupid child's fantasy story!" he yelled back, patience growing short. "How many drinks did you have at Beezel's before getting here? I'd say quite a few to come up with such a drunken delusion as that. Have you also forgotten that you were almost murdered out there in the streets?" his teeth gritted as he came to the end of the lecture. The thought of murder shook Casper, reminding him of Alyssa's fate in the alley. He began to question it before being cut off by the angel. "Your friend was killed by a drakengol. A creature that once was a man but sold his soul to Satan in hopes of reaping the benefits of demonic powers. Satan is a hard mage to please though, and when rejected by him, a soul is destined to live its life as a drakengol and forced to serve the one who would not accept it."

"But why did he kill Alyssa and not me?" Casper asked in sober wonder. "What good was killing an innocent victim?" It was getting harder and harder for him to disbelieve what had been happening recently and he was beginning to think it was real.

"Drakengols are not particularly bright as they lost most of their intelligence in selling their soul. He didn't bother checking for your markings." He replied, pointing to Casper's wrists. "She must've led the drakengol to believe she was the cyspherion somehow and that was proof enough for him. He murdered her on the spot."

"But the knife…?" he asked trailing off.

"Made out of a fang from one of our sky drakes, it is incredibly sharp and strong. He left it there to boast. We were both searching for the cyspherion and I had been watching you. When he killed Alyssa, he believed he had gotten to you first…" Wyburn slowed his words down. "So I couldn't protect you." He finished, making Casper suddenly feeling awkward with Wyburn.

"That angel…my mother, said something about vampyres." He said, trying to shift the uneasy feelings in the room. "Crosspien I think?" This made Wyburn laugh a little.

"The Crosspien Vampyres are merely a myth," Shaking his head, he tried to suppress the laughter while staring at the ground. "Your mother believed so deeply in them though. She swore when the war ended, she would find them. They are said to be the oldest living creatures. They are a neutral party that has committed their lives to retaining knowledge. If found, they are capable of answering any question." Wyburn shifted his gaze from the floor to where he was standing. "They don't exist. It would be a waste of time." He continued in response to Casper's wondering stare. He turned away from the young man and gazed out a nearby window. "It'll be daylight soon. You'll be safe in here, but you should get some rest." He turned around, smiling at Casper. "Goodnight." A bright flash emitted from Wyburn, staggering Casper backwards to trip into a pew. He sprawled backwards onto the wooden surface and lost conciseness. His eyes blinked shut, filled with the vision of Wyburn's self satisfied smile.

Chapter 9

The old church trembled at the sound of its bells. Their reverberating songs woke Casper out of his deep sleep. Feeling refreshed, he climbed up to a sitting position in the pew. His eyes studied the room around him. A few scattered families occupied the church as they sat in silent prayer. After a moment it occurred to him that he had slept through his birthday and into Sunday. As the last church bell's echo gave way to silence, everyone turned their heads to look up towards the church alter.

"Greetings and welcome to the church my children." The all too familiar voice caught Casper's attention as its soothing sound floated about. He watched the elderly Wyburn walk slowly towards the podium. Dressed in vestments, he looked just like any other pastor to Casper. "I think we have some new faces in our congregation today." He looked to where Casper was sitting and gave an exaggerated wink in his direction. "We should welcome all those who seek to learn our knowledge from us."

"Crazy old man," Casper grumbled, rising from the pew. He walked slowly toward the back of the church, feeling the burning eyes of disappointed stares on his broad back. Before reaching the door, he saw a pile of old hymnals and Bibles stacked haphazardly into piles. With a quick step he kicked the piles over. The books sprawled across the floor into an unorganized mess.

"Hail Zeus!" he yelled while turning around and pumping both fists into the air with his middle fingers extended. He retained this pose until he had pushed the door out of the way with his back and walked out. Just before the door closed behind him, Casper heard Wyburn introducing a new preacher. He hurriedly made it down the stairs and into street. Bending down to inspect the asphalt, he could clearly see where the largest hell hound had been. Blood from the banker's corpse had splattered about as it was thrashed about without mercy. A little pile of bone shrapnel lay around a rather large blood patch. He assumed the hound had gotten tired of waiting and settled there for his little snack. Casper grimaced at the disgusting display around him. Perhaps he hadn't been dreaming after all. He had once thought that he was too smart to believe the forces of good and evil had battled and created him, but his doubts were wearing thin.

The door of the church opened, spilling sounds of mass into the open air. He grunted in disappointment. He had waited too long in the street and now Wyburn was about to reprimand him with more of the strange religious beliefs.

"Get back in there and behave yourself," the angel snarled as he jumped down the steps with ease.

"You're not my real father," Casper said defiantly while looking away. "I don't have to listen to you."

The angel lunged menacingly into the street and grabbed Casper by his neck, forcing him to lean backwards until he was staring at the sky.

"You will listen to me. I'm the best you've got." He spit into Casper face. "Don't you ever even think about defying GOD again. What would compel you to do that?"

"I thought you worked for Zeus. I was merely supporting the cause you damn hypocrite." Casper shot back, trying to slap Wyburn's hold off of him.

"I'm aligned with Zeus. I praise GOD. Don't forget it. Without Him, we wouldn't even exist." He released his grip on Casper, making the bent man stumble backwards. Casper rubbed his neck vigorously as he stared venomously back at Wyburn. Slowly walking backwards, he kept his eyes on the aged angel and neglected to watch where he was going. A crunching noise beneath his shoes reminded him of the grotesque pile under his shoe. He instantly moved away from the bone pile out of respect for whatever was left of the corpse. The street had been thoroughly coated in blood though, and after a moment of dancing around the stains, he gave up and settled for standing among the bloody patches.

"So if these battles have been going on all this time, why hasn't anyone seen them? They should've been all over the news," he sneered.

"The war of good and evil is clouded to humans by GOD in protection. He wishes no innocent human casualties, so everyone associated with a battle is taken into a shrouded fog, almost like a ghost world."

"Whatever, listen I don't need your religious crap. I've gotten by on my own so far and I think I can handle myself." Casper turned and started walking down the street.

"The only reason you've survived for so long is because no one knew who you were. We couldn't find you. Until yesterday, your powers of good and evil have been negating each other, making you just like any other human. Once you reached your twenty first birthday however, they were able to stabilize and now you're going to start sticking out like a sore thumb."

Casper continued down the street. While trying to brush Wyburn away from him, he suddenly remembered his hurt leg. Looking down he could see that there were no longer any scratches underneath the shredded bloody pant leg. Slightly amazed by the quick healing, he was startled by Wyburn's voice over his shoulder.

"See that, your subconscious mind is already using the powers to your advantage. It healed itself while you were sleeping." Casper merely scoffed at the remark and pushed Wyburn away with his shoulder blade.

"Get back here!" Wyburn demanded as he once again walked down the street away from him. "We're not done here." Wyburn ran to catch back up to the defiant man, but stopped short as they turned a corner. Debris littered the street that Casper had taken to escape the hellish mutts. The two gaped at the destroyed road as memories surfaced of the actions that had happened to him only two nights ago.

"I need to get going," Wyburn said quickly when he caught sight of the policemen patrolling the wrecked road. "The police force can be a dangerous enemy and an even more dangerous ally." With that, the old angel turned and hurried back towards the church, avoiding the roving eyes of the cops. Casper made his way slowly down the road, turning his head in every direction to take in the entire scene. Total destruction had swept this part of town as the creatures chased down Casper. He now he could see what was left in its wake.

On his right side, Casper heard the gurgling sound of a fire hydrant. He turned to see water springing lazily up from only the bottom half that had stuck in the ground and flowed down the sidewalk. The top half of it was embedded in a nearby concrete wall. All along the street and sidewalk, the pavement had been cracked methodically in conjunction with the beasts' steps. Street signs had been strewn all over the road, some twisted into bizarre shapes. He bent down to examine one and ran his fingers down the pole, feeling the teeth marks that had been gouged into it. One of the hounds must have used his jaws to tear it out of the ground in order to get it out of its way. Standing back up, he continued observing the total destruction about him. A few cars had been bashed in and some were pushed out of the way and onto the sidewalk. A little more walking brought him back to the truck he had leapt over. The automobile was still smoldering from its previous inferno. As Casper circled it in inspection, an officer approached him.

"You see any of this happen?" questioned a professional tone.

"No, what happened?" Casper asked slowly.

"Don't know. There are only two witnesses so far. One was driving this truck. Claims a herd of gigantic black and red dogs wreaked havoc down the street." He glanced down at the clipboard in his hand. "And one woman, whose entire downstairs was destroyed, claimed a young man ran through her upper floor and tried to get a free show of her taking a bath?" He ended his statement almost in a question, as if he could not believe what he had been saying."

"Well why hasn't any of this been cleaned up yet?"

"We're working as fast as we can. Whatever did this did a hell of a job on our town. We'll be lucky to have everything done within the next year." He waved his arm around to indicate the entire area and then the cop's eyes narrowed down as he tried to study Casper's face. "Are you from around here?"

Casper didn't bother answering the officer's question as he had become preoccupied on debating an easy way to leave the scene. When the officer's hand had waved around the streets, Casper had caught a glimpse of his wrists. A pentagram was scrawled on the skin but unlike Casper's cross, it was drawn on with an ordinary pen. Casper figured this man was attempting to sell his soul to Satan and being around him was a bad idea. He covered his wrists by clamping them firmly to his sides. Casper's awkward stance only served to catch the older man's attention though.

"Is something wrong?" he asked, pointing to Casper's stiff arms. "You look awfully tense right now, is everything alright?" He could almost feel the cop's hazel eyes burning through him and searching his soul for its dark secrets. Casper's eye began to twitch slightly with worry as he racked his brain for an excuse to move away. The balding head of the cop leaned forward and his nostrils flared whenever he breathed, trying to intimidate the cyspherion.

"I'll be fine." He mumbled finally. "Just sore, I need a new mattress for my bed." Without waiting for an answer, he turned around and starting walking briskly away from the wrecked truck and the officer. "Hope you find the psychos who did this!" He yelled out.

Continuing his walk down the road, it wasn't long before the lady's house came in view. Looking at its dilapidated shape, Casper couldn't help but chuckle a little as he remembered what the officer had said about him trying to get a free show. He walked by with his smirk but the sight of the lady in the front yard looking around in disbelief at the mess made him avert his face so as to not be recognized. A steady crackling sound emitted from a telephone pole that had been broken in half. It was lying in Casper's path, causing him to stop lest he trip right over it. He walked cautiously around it, avoiding the electrical wires as they snapped ferociously about with power.

He sunk deep within his thoughts and let his sub consciousness guide him back to Beezels. As the path of destruction came to an end, he looked back to where he had been and sighed at the desolate scene. He felt for the door frame and let himself into the bar, trying to shake the dismal scene from his eyes. Walking throughout the room, he could see news being broadcasted on the outdated and beat up television set near Noel at the bar. Everyone in the area seemed intently fixated on the small blinking screen. Stumbling to the bar, he could hear the distinct voice of the girl from the channel seven news.

"Although unconfirmed what actually caused this disastrous mess, there have been several reports from eyewitnesses claiming that a pack of wild dogs were chasing a man down the street." The girl on the television couldn't help but to make the witnesses sound more than a little insane with their unbelievable recounts. She walked through the destroyed streets where Casper had been only minutes ago. "We're on day two here and the Heresen Police Force are doing everything in their power to solve this very bizarre mystery. This is Kaylee O'Donnell with the morning news. We'll be back at four with more details and now back to Kevin." The television switched back to the newsroom and everyone in the room quickly lost interest in it. As the crowd slowly dissipated throughout the bar, Casper could make out the form of the closest friend he had.

"Hey blondie, you been here this whole time?" He shouted to the other side of the room. Gasping in shock, Justine turned around at his voice. She ran and jumped with an embrace into his expecting arms.

"No you dumb nut." She answered before burying her head into his chest. "I went to your house when you didn't come back. I've been so worried that something happened to you. Where have you been? Have you seen what happened out there?"

"Slow down, girl. I had to go take my friend's pets for a walk and feed them." He answered. "Of course I saw it. I don't think there's any way I could've missed it." He paused to look at the people scattered about. "What's the world coming to, blaming all this destruction on a couple of dogs? Such sick and twisted people we live with. But enough of that, let's get back home. I'm sick of hearing about the destruction" He pushed Justine away from his chest but held onto her wrist as he led her to the door. They forced themselves through the door and into the bright light outside. Walking briskly, Casper released her hand and stayed ahead of Justine as she tried her best to keep up. Approaching his home, he slowed down to survey the area. Unable to spot any plausible danger, he walked up to his house and grabbed a loose piece of wood from his porch. The door creaked as he pushed the front door open and slowly walked through, searching for intruders. His search came up unsuccessful and he finally came to rest in the living room. Slumping down into his couch, he heaved a sigh of relief and let his eyelids block off his vision.

"Alright tough guy, what's going on?" Justine asked as she jumped onto the empty spot next to him. "Something's going on here and you know what it is." She grabbed him by the face and pulled it close to hers as she spoke, causing him to open his eyes.

"You're going to think I'm crazy." He said through pursed lips. Feeling uncomfortable with her hands on his face, he grabbed them softly and slid them off his face so he could speak with ease. "But I need to tell someone and you're probably my best bet." He sighed, trying to prolong having to tell the girl of what strange events had happened to him the past few days. "Well," he started, "Let's start at the beginning."

Casper told the blonde his terrifying ordeals and she listened intently as fascination and silence kept her lips sealed. She had no reason to distrust her friend, so had no choice but to believe what he was saying. Staying silent throughout the story, she listened until the sun had sunken low on the horizon and he had finally finished. They spent the rest of the night debating what it all meant and who to trust. They kept each other awake into the wee hours of night, only claiming a few hours of sleep before having to wake up for work the next morning.

Chapter 10

The dusty antique shop was cluttered with curios and odd assortments of furniture. The moving truck had taken off to clean out a few select houses around town. Peter had recovered from his illness and once again was able to work for Jesse. It was perfect timing as one of the cashiers had needed the day off. Knowing about Justine's reliability, Jesse gave her a job on the spot and left Casper in charge of training her to run the shop.

Casper leaned back in his chair as he watched her explore the untidy shop. Stepping throughout the store, she examined its contents. A glass tank in the corner caught her attention and she made her way over to it. A large stick stuck up through the shavings covering the bottom of the tank. The shavings quivered with oddly erratic movement. She leaned in closer to see mice running around inside.

"Jesse keeps pet mice in his store?" she asked as she tapped the glass to get the rodents' attention.

"Nope." He answered nonchalantly. As if on queue, a giant reptilian head shot out of the shavings and hissed at the tapping hand. She jumped back in fright and let out a little shriek. "He keeps a pet snake in his store." He finished, chuckling slightly at her reaction. "The mice are his lunch."

She glared at the spotted head as its jet black eyes sized her up. The staring contest continued for only a few moments before Justine backed up a step and walked away to search through the rest of the shop. Her search came to an old bookcase filled with deteriorating books. It had been collecting dust for years and only when she wiped her hand down the spines did the names become visible. The outdated volumes of writing had worn down and she could barely make out the words on each book. Intrigued with the names that she could make out, she began pulling the books out and pouring over the ancient knowledge held within.

"I think those belonged to some guy that died down the street from here, about ten years ago," Casper yelled from the register as he looked lazily back at the ceiling. It had been a slow day with no customers, so Justine was able to learn how to run the shop almost immediately and now they lacked chores to do. In her boredom, Justine had begun to explore and familiarize herself with the store. *A Unique Antique* was not far from Jesse's house and the area proved to be a poor placement for business. Not many people with money wanted to venture into that part of town to visit the store and the local families had very little spending cash.

The bell above the door rang, alerting the two that someone was entering. Looking up, they saw a woman with a young boy come inside, holding hands. They immediately began perusing the wares in interest.

"Let me know if I can get you anything." Casper yelled emotionlessly to the customers before turning back to the ceiling. The woman snorted at the offer and released the boy's hand, who squealed in glee as he ran off to wreak havoc. "Make sure your kid doesn't touch anything," he continued unenthused, "You break it, you buy it."

"What is that, your company motto?" the woman sneered. "My child is very careful and intelligent. At least he's smarter then you."

"You're probably right," he chuckled, still staring up. "But our motto is 'We only want to sell you a genuine antique.'"

"I don't get it." She said after pausing for the motto to sink in. Casper turned his head to look at the voluptuous lady as he smirked.

"That's what we count on."

The lady heaved a sigh of exasperation at his response and turned towards the old furniture scattered about. Justine's attention had been caught by the customers but she now lost interest and turned back to the bookcase, opening each book and letting the dust fly out of it, coughing periodically. The store sat in silence that was only broken by coughing or the customers' rude scoffs at the store's contents.

"Look, I think you should see this," Justine stated as she picked the book off of the table she was using to study on and brought it over to him. He tried to look at the book but a hissing sound from the corner broke his concentration.

"Hey, get away from that, it's not for sale!" He yelled to the little boy who had been antagonizing the angered snake trapped in its glass prison. The boy looked up in shock and shied away from it.

"Don't yell at my boy!" The large woman snapped, walking towards the register with a few tacky knickknacks in her hand. "Now I want to buy these, but the prices on them can't be right, they're way too much."

"First of all, tell your son to get away from our snake, kibbles." The woman looked over to where her boy was standing, still interested in the creature inside. Casper took this momentary distraction to gracefully slide the business telephone from on top of the counter down to one of the compartments underneath.

"Don't tell me how to raise my child you imbecile," she answered, turning around, totally oblivious as to what Casper had just done. "He's at least ten times smarter than you. He knows what he's doing." Casper merely shook his head and looked at the items she held to her chest. The items she chose he could only assume were the worst statues and dinnerware Jesse had put on display. She dumped them onto the front counter for Casper to examine. He turned each item about in his hand, studying it unnecessarily and looking for each price tag. After a moment of looking he finally looked up.

"Well I agree with you." He said sarcastically, "These things are grossly overpriced. I would only pay..." Casper paused to ponder a price for her to agree with. About to answer, he was cut short by a sharp shriek. Everyone looked over to the snake tank where the boy was standing. They looked on with terror as he pulled his arm out of the glass aquarium while yelling in pain.

"Oh my poor baby," the woman said with instant concern.

"Ma'am, I told him not to play with the snake, that's a Massasauga rattlesnake." Horror stained her face at the sound of the name rattlesnake. She turned a sickly pale color and ran over to her little boy to examine the bite marks on his arm.

"We've got to do something!" She yelled. "He's been poisoned! Why would you leave a dangerous animal where a child can get at it?"

"Ma'am, you better get him to a hospital, that poison's incredibly lethal. He'll die soon without medical attention!" Casper exclaimed with fake sympathy.

"My car's at the garage being fixed. Call an ambulance quickly!" she squawked at Casper. "Oh my poor, poor baby," she cooed, turning back to the boy and pulling him close to her. "It's ok, mommy's here, nothing's going to happen." The boy only whimpered a pain induced reply.

"We have no phone here. Our service has been out for weeks, ever since we sold our antique phone collection and cancelled out our number. I want to help but there's nothing I can do." The woman turned back and looked at Casper's face as he tried his best to look worried for the young child.

"I saw one of your company vans parked next to the building. You have to take us to the hospital right away!" She demanded.

"Well, I'd love to. It's just I can't leave my post. It's company policy. My boss would kill me if I took off in the van without his permission. It looks like you better hurry him to the hospital by foot. From the looks of his face, you don't have much time." The boy's face had long since turned a sickly white and had started to slump against her body, losing the balance to stand.

"You're a heartless animal!" Yelled the woman as she picked the boy up in her arms and ran to the front of the store. "Your boss is going to hear about this! Oh honey, don't worry, its all going to be alright." She said just before pushing out the door and running down the street, carrying the child in her arms.

"What the hell is your problem?" Casper turned to see Justine's face filled with rage. "That poor boy is poisoned and you refused to help out? Just because he wouldn't listen to you is no excuse to let someone possibly die!" Casper, unable to hold his solemn facial expressions, burst out in laughter, confusing his blonde friend.

"Kibbles is an eastern fox snake. Its bites are painful, but not lethal." He explained, finally able to control his breathing and stop his laughter. "They'll find out once they get to the hospital. Maybe she'll learn to listen to the ignorant cashiers next time." He finished, raising an eyebrow. Justine looked at him with fake anger, but his smirking face made her crack into a smile.

"You really are a heartless animal, you know that don't you?" she said, grinning at his ruse and grabbing the phone to put back on the counter. Slamming it back in place, she moved her hand to Casper and smacked his head with her open palm before returning it to her side. "Don't scare me like that again." The two looked at each other with grins plastered across their face.

"Alright, what did you want me to see?" He asked, turning back to a serious tone. Looking back down to the book, he read the title aloud. "Myths of Ancient Mexico." She grabbed the pages and flipped through them, landing on one. Excited at her find, she pointed enthusiastically to the tattered page she had opened to, labeled Crosspien Vampyres.

"The Crosspien Vampyres are an ancient race of Vampyres that dwell in Central Mexico among the ancient ruins of the Aztecs." He said, reading the page to himself. "They spend their lives collecting knowledge and contain more information than any other race in existence. Neutral in diplomacy, they will help any creature who seeks them out for aid." He furrowed his brow as he struggled to read the words from the weathered book. "The cavern they dwell in is well protected and finding is nigh impossible. If they wish to be found, they will allow themselves to do so. Those who wish to gain their knowledge must be prepared to sacrifice in trade much like the Aztecs once did." Casper looked up. The page was ripped and the remaining information was missing. "Where's the rest of it?" he asked with slight anger in his lips.

"I don't know, it wasn't in the book. That doesn't matter anyway. Isn't that what you told me about last night?" She asked. "Maybe there's more truth to those stories than you think." She looked at him with a wondering grin and he returned it with a thoughtful somberness. "Did you see any other books in there?" he asked with sudden interest in the old bookcase.

"No, they're mostly just cook books or fantasy stories." The two stared at each other until they realized what she had said.

"Maybe they're less fantasy than you think." He jumped up with excitement, grabbing the book and leaping over the counter. Pushing his way across the store, he raced Justine to the collection of books. Grabbing books two at a time, the two friends began looking frantically for any book that could possibly be related to the recent occurrences that had happened to Casper. Looking only for a short period of time, he suddenly felt a wave of nausea sweep over him. The quaint surroundings of the antique store had once made him feel comfortable but now the feeling of safety washed away. Only a second passed before he figured out what was wrong. Dropping the books in his hand and turning around, he could see Ben's outline in one of the front windows of the store holding a stick-like object in his hand. Unable to yell a warning out fast enough, Casper lunged himself backwards while kicking the back of Justine's unsuspecting knees.

"Take cover!" He screamed as he landed on his back and watched Justine stumble by his unseen motions. She fell backwards just as the sounds of a shotgun being fired ricocheted throughout the store. The sound of Ben cocking the mighty gun could be heard over the noises of shattering glass as the window fragments hit the ground. He fired three more shells angrily in the general direction of Casper. As the pellets hit the books above, they destroyed the old tomes, making shredded papers rain down around them both. Breathing in quick, shallow breaths, Casper looked over to where Justine was lying. Blood gushed from a bullet wound in her shoulder. She tried in vain to cover it with her hand as her mouth gasped for breath.

"It's ok," She murmured. "Just a stray shot, I'll be fine." Unconvinced, Casper felt anger flood through his blood stream. Justine had taken care of him since he was a child and now she was lying in a pool of her own blood, wounded by the one man he hated more than he could have ever imagined. Looking up at him, Justine could see Casper's eyes change from his natural blue to a deep red. "Casper, calm down, I'll be fine." She gasped as his eyes turned completely red. He looked down at his wrists and noted that the tattoos were glowing the same mysterious red color to match his eyes. He shifted his gaze back up to her who looked back in shock at his transformations. Another load of pellets flew by Casper's head, making him snap his head around to where Ben stood.

"Damn," Ben cursed outside the window as he started hastily reloading the empty shotgun. Without thinking, Casper stood up and turned to where the preoccupied man was standing. Once Ben realized that there was action occurring inside the store, he looked up with a cautious stare. His smile faded into shock as he saw Casper's new glowing state. With rage burning through every vein in his body, Casper raised his hand until his palm pointed directly at the assailant's face. With a surreal concentration, he let all of the rage in his body flow unchecked into the raised arm. A flaming ball shot forth from the outstretched hand and sped towards Ben's unprotected face. With sudden alarm, Ben dove out of the way but was too slow to escape the fiery inferno. As the fire reached his skin he screamed in pain and smacked his hands against his head, trying to put the painful flames out. Unsuccessful, he started running down the street away from the antique shop and towards the safety of the town. Once relieved of Ben's company, Casper's eyes turned back to his blue eye color and his wrists ceased to glow. Looking back to the ground, he saw that Justine was now squeezing her shoulder in attempt to slow the bleeding and curb the pain.

Battling to gain control of her breath, she tried to gasp to him that she was alright but failed. He knew better than to listen to her pretending to be fine anyway and bent down next to her. His hand slid softly across her body, sliding her hand out of the way and off of the bleeding wound. Without knowing exactly what he was doing, Casper started to let his love for the woman swim through his body. He could feel total sedation as the two went into a trance. Justine stopped bleeding under his hand and her arm began to heal. He slowly brought his eyes from her shoulder to look at her face. As they stared at each other, both realized that no amount of dreaming could explain what had just happened to the both of them in the store.

He moved his hand slowly from her bloody shoulder. Feeling slightly groggy from healing her, he had to use great effort to move his arm back to his side. They sat in silence as both tried to formulate words that could match the shock they felt within themselves. Before either one could break the silence, a paper came fluttering down to land between the two. Casper picked it up to examine what it said. The shotgun had demolished most of the paper, but the top of the page still stood out and Casper mouthed out the title. "Crosspien Vampyres." They looked at each other for a moment before Casper jumped up to his feet and made his way to the front cash register. Grabbing a piece of paper and a pen, he hastily scrawled a note and stuck it next to the register then shoved debris out of his way as he started heading for the front door.

"Where are you going?" She called after him.

"To Mexico, I need to get some answers!" he yelled back to her. "Go back to my house, and don't let anyone in. I left a note telling Jesse where you are. He'll come and take care of you while I'm gone." Casper stopped to take one last look back to his closest friend as a tear formed in his eye. "I'd take you with me, but it's too dangerous and Jesse is the best protection around. Don't worry, I'll be back soon. " With that, Casper turned and kicked the front door out of his way, disappearing into the sunlight outside.

Justine watched the figure pass by the broken window, shedding a few tears as she saw him sprint away. After a minute of sitting on the floor to let everything sink it, she pushed herself up onto her feet. She knew Casper was right. She had to get out of there. As she walked toward the door, she picked up a metal pipe resting nearby. With heavy thoughts on her mind, she opened the door and made her way onto the street towards Casper's house.

Chapter 11

Wheezing from his run, Casper arrived at the Heresen airport. His run had taken him all the way from the antique shop to the outer reaches of town where the airstrip was located. Bracing one hand against the stone building, he finally caught his breath just outside of the airport. Passing crowds looked on in confusion as the sweating cyspherion regained control of his lungs.

Finally able to breathe normally, he slid his hand off of the smooth wall and checked out the status of his appearances. Brushing himself down, he quickly groomed his body so as to look slightly less of a mess. He walked through the sliding glass door and stopped only momentarily as they slid closed behind him. Stepping quickly through crowd, Casper roughly pushed his way through the irritated lines.

"Hey wait your turn." A statement from a rather grotesque man made him turn around and stare at the person behind him. The impatient guy stared up with anger as he balled his fingers into a fist. Extending his thumb, he used it to point toward the end of the line. "C'mon, pronto, let's go!" he growled after a moment as he glared back at him.

Casper's somber face turned to a smile as malicious thoughts crossed his mind. Walking to where the man stood, he continued to grin as his arm launched a swift fist into the man's stomach. With a disgruntled look he doubled over in pain as words were forced through clenched teeth.

"What…what the hell m-man." He huffed, clutching his gut and staggering around. "Try th-that again and I-I'll break, ugh, your freaking arms!"

Shrouded in the protection of the crowd, any official standing around was unable to see what had happened or didn't bother to respond. Heresen was notorious for fights as it was and it was not unusual to have unruly people get into a disagreement, even in an airport. Casper's grin widened at the man's poor attempt to threaten him. His response consisted of another swift punch, this time to the man's temple, knocking him over in the process. Lying beaten at Casper's feet, he could only roil in pain and whimper silently.

"Anyone else here have a problem?" he asked as the lowered edges of his lips dipped into an even more threatening demeanor. The entire group moved away, making a path for him to walk through. Slight apprehension marked each face as they shied away from him while he walked to the front counter. "I didn't think so." He added, turning around to address the group. "Thank you for your time."

The woman at the counter gave Casper a superficial smile as he strode over to her.

"What can I help you with today?" She asked in an upbeat tone. Casper in turn, closed his eyes to slits and glared at the girl as she stared back with her fake smile.

"Knock it off," he growled, finally cutting the silence between the two of them. "No one's ever that happy, especially at their job."

"I love my job here. Everyone does. It's a great place to work."

"Yeah right, we both know you're counting the minutes until your shifts over. Whatever, fine just tell me when the next flight's boarding for Mexico."

"What part of Mexico sir?" she refused to surrender her fraudulently cheerful countenance as she spoke.

"What the hell. Wherever, just get me as close to the Aztec ruins as you can."

"Well we have a plane leaving for Mexico City in about half an hour, will that do?"

"Yes, thank you."

"Alright," She turned to the computer in front of her, "We only have coach left and I'll need to see some ID."

"I don't want a ticket you stupid whore!" he yelled, slamming closed fists onto the counter. "I just wanted to know when it was taking off and which plane it is." Anger fumed from his lips as he battered words against her unmoving complexion. "Now which plane is taking off for Mexico?"

"Gate twelve, the airline is Seventh Hope, sir." She responded, slightly bewildered. The two stood motionless for just a moment longer before Casper turned his back on the girl. She took this moment to break her smile and let loose an unnecessarily larger frown than needed. He took a step away from the counter as she raised her middle finger to his back. Without moving any other part of his body, he swung his arm back to grab the protruding finger before she could retract it. His face resumed the malicious smile he had previously shown the man on the ground as he spun back around to meet her scowl. He chuckled a little while bending the finger to one side. She let out a little gasp and started bashing his hand in a futile attempt to get free. He continued twisting the tiny finger with his powerful wrist, enjoying the yelping sound she made with every twist. Flitting movement caught the edge of his vision. He broke his concentration on the airport worker and looked to where the movement was coming from. Three strong looking security guards were running from somewhere in the back towards the counter.

Shifting his gaze back to the counter, he saw the girl smiling through her pain. With her hand resting somewhere under the counter, Casper realized that she had set off a silent alarm.

"Damn," he muttered under his breath while releasing the reddened finger from his grasp. In a fluid motion he turned around towards the door and pressed his foot against the bottom of the counter. Using the surface to push off, he leapt into a sprint and vigorously pumped his feet against the ground, racing the security guards for the front door.

"That's the guy." "Don't let him get away!" and "He hit me, that ass hit me!" were all protests he heard around him as he shouldered through the crowd which had converged back into a mass all around him, hoping to block his attempt of escape by impeding his retreat. Once he saw what they were doing, he no longer settled for using his shoulders and began throwing punches at any flesh that he could land a blow on. He heard the sounds of guns being used not too far behind. The guards were taking no chances on the possibility of Casper being a terrorist and planned to take him down by any means necessary. Luckily for him though, the humans around him served as excellent shields and he used them to his advantage while ducking and weaving through them.

Their attempts to stop him only served to move themselves closer to him and become disposable protection. Finally on the other side of a human wall, he smashed through the remaining few people to sweet freedom. A shriek from the floor let him know that he had knocked a nearby woman over. Uncaring, he sped towards the closed glass doors. Too far away from the motion sensors, the glass doors stayed shut as he ran on. One of the guards wasn't far behind and his close proximity caused sweat to bead across Casper's forehead. The sturdy doors refused to move as he started running even faster. Hoping it would not hurt too much, he dove towards the door and closed his eyes, preparing for the impact that never came. A whoosh of air surrounded Casper as the doors flew open, letting him glide out into the open air. He landed in a roll, taking only a second to spring back up to his feet. Looking back, he watched the doors as they closed, framing the pursuing guards in thick panes of glass. Still stuck in the havoc filled crowd, they staggered about, trying to get free. Those who had tried to stop Casper now served to impede the guards and give him time to escape. He motioned obscenely towards them before running off.

Turning around a corner, he skidded to a stop. The airport runway was completely surrounded by a chain link fence with barbed wire adorning its top. Without a second thought he jumped onto the fence and began climbing the chain links. About halfway up the fence he could hear the glass doors sliding open, letting the security guards out to continue their pursuit. He quickened his pace until he reached the fence top. He only had one chance to escape now and took it. Channeling rage through his veins he could feel the demonic blood flow through him. He released his grip on the fence with one hand and pointed the palm towards the barbed wire inhibiting his climb. With all of the energy he could muster, he forced anger into his palm, transforming it successfully into a ball of flame. As the shrieking fire left his palm, it incinerated a portion of each of the two wires before flying freely into the sky. The remaining wire snapped back with a twang as they unleashed their tension. Continuing his climb, he could still feel the residing heat that remained from the fireball. The top bar of the fence had melted slightly, giving him a groove to hold on to and pull himself up. The guards still hadn't caught up to him as he climbed up and perched on the fence. Throwing himself forward into a freefall, he landed soundly in the airport's take off zone. His feet hit the ground and allowed his knees to absorb the impact before scrambling across the pavement to hide around the side of the building. He pressed his body against the wall and listened as the guards ran by the fence. Perplexed at his disappearance, they continued running by the fence and off down the road, oblivious to the barbed wires hanging down.

Casper, invigorated by his close encounter, pulled himself off of the wall and looked away from the disappearing guards. His eyes searched frantically around the take-off strips. Only a few planes were scattered throughout the zone but it was not surprising as Heresen was not a central location for flights. The few employees working in the zone were milling about or using vehicles to transport fuel, luggage, or passengers to their flights. Looking down toward his feet, he saw a pair of bolt cutters leaning on the wall just next to him. Although an odd tool to have just lying around, he had no time to question its purpose. He only knew that there was a flight to catch.

A large elaborate seven was painted across a plane parked at gate twelve. Clearly seen from across the strip, Casper knew he had to find a way across the zone to the plane before it took off. A luggage cart came close to the wall and he seized his chance. He ran to the end of it, ducking down so as to not draw attention and squeezed in between the bags to settle for a ride. He bumped around for a bit until the cart changed direction. As it turned to the left, he leaped out and took cover behind a wheel from a neighboring jet. Guards were patrolling the runway close by and running to plane seven would be impossible for now. They talked for what he feared would be too long. As seconds droned on to minutes, he stared impatiently on, awaiting any opening. A sudden noise near the building caught their attention and they ran off to attend to any problems that might have arisen. The only chance he had, he sprung off and ran to the plane's side. The roar of the engine shook him as it began it's take off procedure. He could already feel the metallic giant beginning to move. The nearest wheel started rolling by him as he ran next to it. He reached up with both hands and grappled onto the landing gear as it rolled by. He rode it down the runway, watching objects pass by slowly as the plane picked up speed. The world around him had starting turning deep red as dusk set and shadows lengthened outside. Becoming airborne, the landing gear started retracting into the wheel well, carrying the hitch hiker with it. The patch of fading light closed, plunging him into total darkness.

"Ouch! Damn it man, watch where you going." Sound came from the enclosed compartment as he repositioned himself for more comfort.

"Hey who's there?" He asked, poking around with his feet. A grunting sound responded, closely followed by his feet being grabbed. The stranger stuck within the wheel well roughly pushed his feet away, smashing it into the landing gear.

"Ow, damn it. Wait a second." Casper tried in failure to make out the facial features of the child near him. "Aren't you Enrique's kid?" he asked, suddenly recognizing the voice. The little Hispanic boy took his time in responding.

"Yeah, I got a name though, Poncho. You know me? Then you know why I'm here." Casper shook his head in disagreement. Poncho was fifteen years old but the last time he had seen the child was about six months ago. There was no feasible reason he could surmise as to why the child was jumping flights to Mexico. It occurred to him that he had not said anything and Poncho was unable to see what him shaking his head.

"No, what in God's name are you doing on here? Isn't your father going to be worried?"

"How you know my father?"

"I work with him. It's Casper. But that doesn't explain what you're doing up here."

"I'm going back to Mexico," he said with defiance. "I hate America, it terrible here, man."

"What do you mean? America's the greatest country in the world. You're free to do what you want."

"Yeah, free to do what you want. Thousands of people die for Americans to live in freedom and the proud Americans squander their freedom on fighting each other. You can live in a world where funerals are picketed merely because the soldiers died in battle to help his country." Silence followed as Casper remembered the recent headlines in the newsprints. People of America had recently started demonstrating against soldier's funerals. The gentlemen and ladies were fighting in search of peace throughout the world, seeking out terrorists and destroying their plans to destroy the modern world and take over in a destructive dictatorship.

The soldiers left in high hopes, but too often returned in caskets. Eccentric groups claimed that the country's sins had angered karma and now America was being punished with the soldiers' deaths.

"So what do you suppose then? Disband American armies and let terrorists take us over?"

"No…"

"What do you want then? Impeach our president for doing a poor job?"

"No, Man!" Poncho yelled back. "You're not listenin' to me. The president's doin' an excellent job. I mean we need to be fighting for freedom." The Mexican boy took a short pause to think through his response. "But we shouldn't be takin' freedom for granted. We should be respectin' the soldiers and treating other American's with respect."

"So you're leaving a country then, just because you don't like how freedom's handled? We all have to deal with something in our lives."

"Man," he punctuated his rebuttal with a swift kick to Casper's unsuspecting body, making him cough silently while trying to hold in the pain. "What kind of country we live in that cares more about celebrities then starving kids in third world countries?"

"But what about…"

"Yeah we have food drives and donations. They make us feel real good. We do our part then go home and forget about who we helped. Man we need to start thinkin' bout more than ourselves." He finished in a grunt. Casper kept his thoughts to himself. Perhaps Poncho was right. He had noticed how little people around the country actually cared about each other. The only kindness he had ever seen served to help someone better their station in life.

Silence led to sleep and slumber flowed through the cramped compartment as each one drifted in and out of sleep. It was a long and painful journey in the wheel well as neither one had room to stretch out. Turbulence jolted both stowaways from their dreams as harsh winds blew against the metal giant in hopes of knocking it out of its flight.

"We're calling your father when we land." Casper said after a moment of yawning. "I've got to tell him where you are, so he can come and get you."

"No way, I'm never going back. I'm gonna live with mi familia in Mexico."

"He's going to worry about you. I've got things to do in Mexico and I can't baby sit you while I'm doing it."

"I just told you, my grandparents, they live in Mexico, I'll live with them." Poncho began to get impatient and anger arose in his voice.

"We're calling your parents and that's final!" Casper reprimanded, anger rising to match Poncho's. Poncho pouted as he crossed his arms across his chest. "Not agreeing with me is just going to make this trip more difficult." Silence ensued once again. They rustled a bit around the large landing gear, trying to reposition for more comfort. Sounds, muffled by the walls around them, still found their way down to the compartment. Laughter and talking were accompanied by the clinking glasses on the service tray. Every so often the pilot could be heard making announcements over the speaker system.

Casper drifted back into his daydreams. This was the first time he had ever left Utah and only now realized that he had left his home long behind. He wondered with reserved fear whether Mexico would be like Utah and if he would be able to find the Crosspien Vampyres. The book and Wyburn had claimed them to be mere fables. His journey to Mexico was based solely on his late mother's wishes to seek them out. He left his home state in hopes of learning what his mother had so desperately wanted to teach him. But what if the creatures never existed and he wasted the entirety of his life, however short it may be, searching through the ruins of Mexico.

Poncho could feel Casper's tension as the thoughts swam through his brain. Still mad at him for wanting to send him back to America, he dared not venture any words of comfort or attempt to help the worry ridden man. Instead, the teenager plotted any possible way to escape his fate at the hands of Casper.

The remaining trip went without as much as a groan from either of the hidden passengers. The plane started its descent toward the runway and the landing gear could be felt shifting beneath them, preparing to be lowered.

"Looks like our stop, kid." Casper yelled over the sound of the motors as they started opening the hatch and lowering the gear. The darkness outside gave little light into the chamber. Repositioning themselves to avoid being squashed, they danced around the moving wheel, judging their safety zones by the small light given off by the pale moon. A hefty arm wrapped around the metal structure, holding the wheel as it extended through the small hole. Casper rode the gear into the open space, breathing the fresh night air as it whipped by his face. Looking back up, he could barely see Poncho sitting inside the hole, grinning back at him.

"I don't think so," Casper growled as he lifted his body back towards the boy. Holding his weight on one of the smaller supports, he reached up with his free hand to grab the child's dangling legs as they blew around in the intense wind. With a mighty pull, he dragged Poncho out of the compartment and into the windy skyline. Held only by his leg, Poncho swung helplessly upside down through the strong breeze. They both looked down see the trees below down below them.

"This isn't Mexico City!" Casper yelled in anger. "There's too many trees around!"

"No, it's Harbieno!" Poncho said, fighting the howling winds. "It's nearby Mexico City, but cheaper to land planes and commute. The security is just as strict though." He pointed with a finger towards the landing strip.

"Damn it all the Hell!" Casper yelled. The landing strip was lit with flood lights and standing all around them were men holding assorted rifles and shotguns. Looking down to the trees, he could see the plane was quickly approaching the fence separating the forestry and the paved landing zone. "Well, time to drop in!" Casper hollered toward Poncho.

"What you talkin….Damn!" Releasing his grip on the airplane, Casper let the two fall towards the trees below. Poncho screamed all the way to the treetops. He had always been terrified of heights, but the idea of being back in Mexico had given him the courage to jump the plane and forget his fears until now. Dropping towards possible death made him remember all his past memories as his very life flashed before his eyes.

Branches snapped as the two of them crashed through the top of the forest. Scrambling furiously for handholds, they flailed about in the trees, smashing wood with their bodies. Splintering boughs fell alongside them as they plummeted downwards. A sudden jolt ran through Casper's body as he stopped in midair. Looking down, he saw that his pants had fortunately snagged on a thick branch, stopping his descent just feet from the deadly ground.

Poncho had somehow fallen slower than Casper, perhaps through hitting more branches than him and now flew downwards just near where he was stuck. Throwing out his muscular arms, Casper caught the falling boy and embraced him in a bear hug, stopping his fall and averting death.

"Much obliged," He choked, trying to swallow as he finally resumed breathing.

"No problem." Shaking his body, Casper released the two from the branch and landed safely below among the branches they had broken just moments before. "Well, we need to find a place to spend the night," Casper said. "I don't know much about Mexico, but I know enough that jungles can be dangerous at any time of the day, but at night they're fatal."

The two made a primitive shelter out of the branches and vines lying about. Barely able to squeeze into it, they held each other close. The shelter's natural creation served to camouflage them from the night predators. Knowing that wandering out into the jungle at night would mean death, Poncho reluctantly stayed with Casper, using him as protection from the night. There would be more chances for him to escape in the morning.

"We're still calling your father." Casper said in fact like manner before throwing his arm over Poncho to ensure he would not escape and let sleep take its course.

Chapter 12

Sounds of wildlife flared throughout the jungle floor as morning broke over the horizon. Birds chirped in Casper's ear as he felt Poncho press against his arm, waking him fully up. Stumbling through the makeshift tent, they tore the branches apart as they stood up. The fauna about them shone off a beautiful green color as the sun struck its beautiful surfaces. Casper looked skyward to where they had fallen the night before. He could barely make out the broken trail they had left in their wake during the descent.

"Won't be long before our presence is covered here," Poncho said, rubbing his eyes, "Jungle will make sure of that." He looked back over at his companion who still studied the trees above. "It alright. We gonna go to the town now."

He looked back to where Poncho had sat back down and nodded. "You know your way back to town?"

"Yeah, that's where mi familia is from. We used to live in Harbieno."

"Good, let's go." Casper walked clumsily over to Poncho and grabbed his wrist. With a quick tug he pulled the boy to his feet. Beckoning toward their surroundings, he motioned for him to lead the way. The two began walking through the dense undergrowth towards what Casper could only hope was civilization.

"Are you sure you know where you're going?" Casper asked. Irritation filled his voice as he pushed a branch away from his face. They had been walking for over an hour and his body had long since been scratched by various plants that resisted his passing. A quick pain on his forearm made him instinctively slap it as he yelped at the stinging sensation. A bug darted quickly away from him, triumphant to have survived. Casper stared at the insect as it flew about. It only was able to clear a few feet from him before it burst into a fiery explosion, leaving Casper to wonder if it had been his glaring or his cyspherion blood that had caused its untimely demise. It did cause him to grin a little however as he watched the flaming pieces scatter out.

"What's wrong, not enjoyin' the jungle?" Poncho finally asked, turning around to grin at Casper who eyed the machete in Poncho's hand as he scowled at the boy a few feet in front of him.

"Aren't you supposed to be using that to make a path for us?"

"I'm getting through just fine," he answered, still smiling wickedly. "Not my fault you can't get through."

Casper growled silently at his response as they continued pushing through the dense jungle. It only took a few moments to awaken a cougar napping overhead. Its deadly eyes followed the two as they trespassed through his territory. A tongue slipped through his mouth, wetting his lips. He had not eaten recently and his last meal had only served to whet his appetite. Slinking down the sturdy tree branches, he began to stalk his prey, waiting for the perfect time to pounce.

Meanwhile, just underneath the giant predator, Casper continued to complain openly about their current situation and question Poncho's ability to navigate.

"Shouldn't we be there by now?" He asked in frustration. "How far can the town be from the airport anyway?"

"It only a couple of miles. It would be shorter, but thanks to you, we have to go out of our way." Casper eyed him suspiciously. "There's guards all over the jungle looking for us. Why you think they were on the landing strip, to welcome you?" Casper thought back to the airport. He was careless and the woman at the counter must have given them all the information they needed. "You screwed up at the airport, huh?" He continued, noting the look on Casper's worried face. "It alright, man. I can get us to Harbieno without them finding us." Casper took a few more steps forward before dropping his hand onto Poncho's shoulder, stopping him in his tracks. A feeling much like what he had witnessed in the antique shop once again tore through his body.

"We're not safe here," he whispered in Poncho's ear. "Give me the machete." Poncho, feeling Casper's fear, slowly moved his hand back to hand him the sturdy sword. Casper felt around until his knuckles grasped the sharp tool and calmly pulled it slowly to his side. The cougar sensed the sudden uneasiness and sprang into action. Afraid of losing his meal the beast plunged downwards with his giant claws extended in front of him. A loud growl emitted from his throat as it approached the two men.

Casper turned with perfect reflexes and swung the machete through the air. He felt it strike the predator's torso as the sharp metal sliced through its belly. Not expecting a counterattack, the feline was caught off guard and fell in pain, missing its target only to slam painfully into the jungle floor. Poncho jumped in horror at the sight of its enormous size as it landed just a few inches from his feet. Although not an enormous size, it was still bigger than any cougar he had ever seen.

Casper drew the machete back to his body, watching the cat as blood dripped from the steel blade. The cougar rolled back onto its paws and glared hatefully back at him. Circling around Casper, the beast sized up the cyspherion in search of his best method of attack. Casper swung the machete in warning strikes, letting the cougar know not to try another offensive attempt. Ignoring his warnings, the cougar tensed its tendons in preparation. When he saw the cat crouching, Casper readied himself for another attack. The mighty cat pounced towards him, letting out a scratchy growl and aiming for his face. Casper responded by strafing gracefully out of its way and catching the blade on its powerful paws. The creature yelped in anger as it smashed once again into the ground. The cougar picked himself up once again and turned on Casper.

"Come on, Kitty," Casper said sympathetically, "I don't want to hurt you anymore. Just go ahead and take off." The cougar couldn't understand the human language and it only served to anger him more. He let out a defiant growl as he positioned himself for yet another jump. "Don't, you'll regret it." Answering its body language with words, Casper tried to dissuade the cougar from fighting. Angrier than it had ever been, the animal flew through the air with death on its lips, determined to rip its teeth into Casper's neck.

Casper pointed the machete directly at the cougar and chambered his attack. As it approached him, he thrust the sword forward, stabbing it straight into the furry flank. The soft underbelly of the creature gave little resistance and the growling beast slid down the blade. He could feel the bloody fur brush against his arms as it came to rest on his raised hands. His inhuman strength kept the cougar suspended in midair with the sword as it thrashed helplessly about. The machete twisted in the cougar's stomach as Casper turned his back to it and brought his arms over one shoulder. With all the strength he could muster, Casper pulled the machete straight up over his head. A sickening gush followed the machete as it sliced through the creature's stomach and internal organs. The metal swung through the air, leaving the cougar to fall to the ground. Spasms shook the body as life slowly departed it. A giant gash ran from its midsection up to its right shoulder, spilling the cougar's glistening entrails onto the jungle floor. After a few seconds the carcass lay flat, no longer having life to support it.

Casper nudged the body with his foot, ensuring that it was in fact dead. Satisfied with the results he looked back up to Poncho who looked back with a horrified face, speckled in cougar blood. He had sat motionlessly in the same spot for the duration of the fight paralyzed in terror as soon as the cougar had appeared. "When's the last time you were attacked by a cougar in Heresen?" Casper asked him rhetorically. Shaking the fear from his face, Poncho reached out and motioned for the machete. The man just stared questionably at the boy. With a sudden motion he turned about on his feet and swung blindly in a well placed slash. An extremely large reptilian head had dropped down behind Casper. Venom dripped from its fangs as the snake had prepared for an attack. The machete had taken care of the problem though and he watched the decapitated head sail into the jungle as the slimy body fell to the earth.

"I think I'll just hold on to this," Casper said as he turned back to the boy. Walking over and pulling Poncho to his feet, he motioned to continue their trek in the jungle.

Poncho began leading him once again through the underbrush, this time having as much difficulty as Casper was experiencing before. Casper bent down and plucked a fern from the ground. Wiping it down the blade, he used the plant as a cloth to clean the blood off as he walked. Inspecting the metal surface carefully, he accepted the cleaning job he had just performed and begun to swing it through the jungle growth, making his own path to walk through.

~~~~~~~~~~~~~~~~ , ~~~~~~~~~~~~~~~~ .

Without his machete, Poncho was able to find Harbieno much quicker. They soon walked out of the jungle and into the outer reaches of the town. Barely large enough to even be considered a town, Casper felt like they had walked out of time and taken a trip back to the poverty stricken thirteenth century. He grimaced at the surrounding town's primitive structures.

"Are we going to find a telephone in this place?" Casper asked after a moment.

"Yeah, good luck with that." Poncho laughed.

"Well why do they have an airport then?" he queried angrily.

"Paid by rich overlords to transport tourists cheaply into their five star hotels in Mexico City."

After a year and a half Poncho had finally returned home and nothing seemed more beautiful to him. The townspeople looked up in curiosity at the visitors. The two of them stumbling into town still covered in the cougar's blood should have attracted more attention, but the villagers knew that the jungle was dangerous. They shrugged it of as an average day in the wilderness.

Casper sheathed the machete as best he could inside his belt as he stepped into the village. One girl saw Poncho's face and automatically ran towards him, face shining with joy.

"Poncho!" She yelled running into his open arms. Casper looked at him with a confused face.

"This is Isabella," Poncho answered in explanation. "Mi... novia..." He finished as he looked back down at the girl in his arms, eyes shining. Casper knew only few words in Spanish, but girlfriend was one of them. He smiled at the couple as they continued their embraced.

"So there was more to leaving then just hating America?" he asked rhetorically. His words made him realize that calling Poncho's father would only separate them again and he could see Poncho's face grow hateful at the mention of America. Although he had never been in love himself, Casper had no reason to break the hearts of such a young couple whose love had endeared over a year of not hearing from each other.

"Well I don't think we'll be finding a phone in this pathetic excuse for a town." He turned to look at the couple with a serious look. "It looks like you'll have to be spending some time here until I can bring you back myself." Poncho's face turned from anger to happiness as a smile crept across his lips. "Well, let's see what's in this...town." He finished with distaste in his words. Obviously not happy to be in the town, he was not afraid to show it with emotions. Poncho ignored his tone and started leading him into the town. The village was incredibly small and they reached the town square relatively quickly to join a few local farmers that had come into town to sell their livestock. They pushed into the group, trying to avoid the people trying to sell them living creatures for food.

They passed by a building in better conditions then the rest, even if not by much. Casper stopped to read the sign. The only word he understood was Café. He stared at the sign a moment longer before stopping Poncho and Isabella.

"Hey look at this." He called over to them. "They've got a café. Let's check it out." Pointing his thumb over toward the building, excitement started to light up in his eyes. Poncho began to protest but changed his mind. Shrugging with indifference, he followed him into the dismal building.

Expecting a friendly atmosphere lit with plenty of sunlight, Casper soon learned the Spanish café was the complete opposite. It was as if someone had modeled the café after a Mexican version of Beezel's back in Heresen. He sighed looking around at all the cutthroats lounging about.

"I've got to stop hanging around these spots." He muttered. The counter stood only a few steps inside the door. Casper quickly made his way over to it and addressed the rugged man standing there, while the two lovers followed in tow.

"I'll take a beer." He grimaced, acting as tough as possible. Even though he was used to the current surroundings, he couldn't help but feel out of place in the strange country. The man behind the counter stared at him blankly, causing Casper to turn back toward Poncho.

"Two problems, man." He said. "One, he don't know English." He pointed to the guy who was now preoccupying himself by cleaning an incredibly dirty glass. "Two, this ain't a bar, It's a Café."

"Could've fooled me." He turned back as the man slammed three glasses in front of him. Not questioning it, Casper grabbed a glass and walked to a dirty booth. He sat down quickly and glanced back to the counter. Isabella and Poncho spoke intently to the man in their native tongue. Isabella pulled a small wad of money from her pocket. With a tug, she pulled some of the cash out of the mass and gave it to the burly man before turning and walking away, following Poncho to the booth where Casper sat. They both hastily sat down across from him, placing their glasses on the table. Casper looked down to finally examine the drink in front of him. It contained a strange concoction that he had never seen before and could only surmise that it was a Mexican drink.

"Drink up, it's good." Poncho smiled as he pointed to the glass, indicating that he wanted him to taste it. Casper drew the cup to his lips and took a large swig of the unrecognizable liquid. An instant later it landed on his tongue and burned his taste buds. He swung his head in pain, causing the drink to splash around inside his mouth, bringing pain to every spot it touched. Unable to hold it in, he turned his head and spit the fiery drink from his mouth. He looked back up to see the two kids laughing uncontrollably.

"Gomuvan juice. Made from gomuvas." Poncho coughed, calming down from his hysterical laughter. "Only found around Harbieno. Take a while, but you get used to them." Casper shot an angry glance back at Poncho before taking a smaller sip. Using all of his endurance, he swallowed the vile juice and held back coughing as it swam down his throat and into the stomach. Still looking at the two Mexicans, he smiled proudly and continued to drink the disgusting fluid while withstanding the pain.

The three of them sat awhile in silence, drinking the gomuvan juice. Casper wanted to talk to Isabella and learn more about her, but decided speech would be impossible as she never spoke English only Spanish.

"El muerte de la noche." The sentence caught Casper's attention as it fell over their table from a nearby group. He looked up at Poncho and Isabella, who had also heard it.

"Death of the night," Poncho said, "They talking about a Harbieno myth. If you let your children or livestock wander at night, they disappear and never be seen again." Casper perked up at the sound of the myth.

"Sounds like vampires," he said, trying as hard as possible to sound disinterested in the subject. "They have anything to do with the Aztec ruins?" Poncho looked at him with a contemplative look.

"Vampires? I say more like the cougar you killed in the jungle. They probably crawling all over them ruins. But the village think that there vampire creatures out there." Casper stared at his almost empty glass. Tipping his head back, he brought the drink to his lips and drank down the remainder of the juice.

"Excuse me, but I need to go to the little boy's room." Casper pushed himself up and away from the table. Walking slowly, he could see the people that were once speaking of vampires were now staring at him. Looking down at them in passing, he saw pentagrams scrawled on their wrists with a crude dye. Almost instantly he pulled his wrists to his sides, but was too late. The group had seen his markings and watched him intently in his passing. He could feel their burning gaze all the way to the restrooms.

Pushing the door open, he slid in and let it shut behind him. He quickly gazed around the room. Two stalls stood across the room, crudely built out of old, worn wood. Turning around, he saw a sink behind him, slightly further back than the door and backed by a mirror. To the left of the room stood a low, opened window which allowed a slight breeze into the bathroom. Perfect, he thought to himself. He went to the stall and stepped inside. Slamming the door shut, he grabbed the deadbolt and slipped it shut. He then ducked under the stall door to return to the main room. Running silently, he jumped onto the sink and pressed his back against the mirror.

Just as he leaned against the mirror, the bathroom door creaked open. Casper watched a man enter silently. His eyes turned instantly to the locked stall. Even with his back turned to him, Casper could already recognize him as one of the men with pentagrams on his wrists. He sat nervously in silence as the man approached the stall, pulling a gun from a holster. Casper pushed his leg against the mirror and quietly pulled the machete from his belt. Tensing his body, he watched the man take aim and raise his leg to kick the door open. Before he got his chance to knock the door open, Casper pushed off against the mirror, launching into midair only to use the Mexican as a landing pad. Falling directly onto his back, he wrapped the machete around him and pressed it firmly against his throat. In the same movement, he grabbed the gun from the man's hand and pried it free only to turn the barrel back at the man's head.

"You know where the Crosspien Vampyres are?" The man whimpered at Casper's question. "You're going to bring me to them." He continued whimpering as Casper growled in the man's ear. "You can understand me, I know you can." With that, Casper pulled the machete closer to the man's neck, causing the blade to draw blood. With that, the man nodded sorrowfully. "Good." Casper released his hold on the man and let him drop to the floor. "Come on, out the window!" He barked, pointing at their exit point. The man pulled himself to his feet and stumbled to the window.

"I have a name, you know." He coughed, looking back. "It's Carlos."

"I don't care." Casper growled. Carlos jumped out of the window, followed closely by Casper, who guarded his guide from escaping. It would be a hard time finding the ruins without him, he thought as they disappeared into the jungle. Determined on his goal, Casper forgot completely about Poncho and Isabella who still sat inside.

Chapter 13

Casper had long since grown tired of the jungle noises as they traipsed through the dense growth. They had been traveling for hours with no results. Carlos was getting tired and dogged his steps with every passing second. Not being very athletic, he had to obtain constant encouragement from the flat side of the machete as Casper pushed him on. Fear of death was the only thing keeping Carlos from leading his captor off course. He had been serving Satan faithfully for years. He was only a few days off of asking him for immortality and wasn't about to let Casper stop him. Carlos could take the body once the vampyres were done with him and claim the kill as his own. He smiled wickedly as he thought of the rewards that would coincide with bringing in the cadaver of the cyspherion. No one would know it wasn't him who had personally killed him and it would certainly save him from a fate of becoming a drakengol.

They came to a halt as Carlos stopped short in his tracks, looking down at the ground.

"What is it?" Casper asked, irritated from the jungle hike. The man only pointed down in front him towards a motionless object lying on the earth. Peeking over Carlos' shoulder, he still couldn't get a good enough look so pushed the gaping figure roughly to the side. He instantly recognized the bleeding carcass. The cougar had not been moved from its resting spot. The only scavengers to find it were bugs that were busy feasting on its organs and eye sockets. Casper nudged the head of it, disturbing a group of insects that droned angrily over to a patch of blood to continue their feast.

"Looks dead." He said finally, looking back up to Carlos.

"Yeah whatever the hell did that to him is dangerous," he replied, looking nervously around him. "We need to avoid it at any cost less we suffer its fate." He continued, thrusting his arm in the direction of the dead cougar.

"Too late." Casper's smile reflected in the shining surface of the machete as he waved it slowly about, before pointing it back towards the carcass. "Looks just about right for a blade cut." He said while tracing the blood drenched cut with the machete's tip. Even as he followed the cut, Casper couldn't help but feel as if the cougar had improved, somehow. The organs seemed to have slid back into body and the cut itself appeared to be trying to heal itself. Carlos licked his lips nervously as he watched the blade slide through the air, curving along the cougar's torso. "Now let's get going, unless you want to share his fate." Carlos took a short, apprehensive breath before turning to lead Casper deeper into the jungle. Casper took one more look back, before shaking the feeling from his mind. He had personally killed the cat and knew that it was just the jungle playing tricks on him.

The two marched on for quite a distance in silence, with only the sounds of breaking plants and birds echoing through their heads.

"So, why did you sell your soul to the devil anyway?" Carlos looked up in surprise as Casper pointed to the pentagrams on his wrists. He scowled, turning back to the path he was making.

"Satan hasn't accepted me." He finally answered with a frown. "I still have to prove myself, but the Vampyres told me to follow the satanic path." His lips drew back up into a sadistic smile at the mention of the vampyres.

"And if you didn't listen to them?"

"They would've killed me." Carlos turned around and looked at him. "Just like they'll kill you." His face turned from a smile to a somber look as his stone cold eyes stared through him. Casper pushed the machete into his back, prodding him forward. Carlos took the hint and started walking again, muttering curses in his native tongue. Walking closely behind him, Casper shuddered at what the man had just said. He wasn't sure how true the words were, but he suddenly realized that perhaps going to the Vampyre's den was not the best idea. Driven by his mother's words though, they trudged on despite Carlo's threat.

The jungle began to thin out and ancient stones, carved intricately began occupying the space around them. He could tell they were from the Aztecs as they looked just like pictures he had once seen in a book. With limited learning supplies, Justine had done her best to give him a proper education. One of the books she had managed to get a hold of consisted of ancient civilizations including the Aztecs. Being his favorite book, he had read it until the binding wore down and the pages fell out into a heaping mass.

He fastened his machete securely inside his belt and stroked each stone in passing, finally able to admire the fascinating artwork in person.

"You like them, huh? I used to come down here as kid. All the time I would play around these statues." Casper looked intently at Carlos' back as he told his story, still walking through the thinning jungle. "It was not far from here that they found me. I came out one night and my parents, they told me not to, but I don't listen to them. Well it was dark and I couldn't see. A rogue hell hound was hunting and found me. I ran as fast as I could but was no match for him." He looked back quickly to ensure that Casper was still paying attention. "I ran all the way to the caverns, which we were forbidden to go. There, they found me and gave me a choice. I could go back to face the hell hound, stay there and be their blood feast, or join the legions of Satan."

"I thought the Crosspien Vampyres were neutral?" Casper asked inquisitively. "Why would they want you to join forces with evil?"

"Because," he hissed in pride, "They know everything, including the superior side." Casper declined to respond to his remark and just continued walking, still studying each carving closely.

A clearing, sparsely cluttered with rocks and formations that once belonged to Aztec culture slowly appeared ahead. They burst through and looked around at the area around them.

"We're here."

"I thought they lived in ruins, these are just statues and pillars." He walked around, looking at each piece with appreciation while searching for the vampyres' domicile. Carlos pointed towards rocks jutting from the ground.

"No, that's just a myth. Just because they once lived with the Aztecs doesn't mean they gonna live in the ruins. They lived in a cavern underground, nearby the temples. They've lived there the whole time. That's why they're considered a myth. No one knows about them under there. Everyone searches the ruins but no one checks the caves." Casper began to walk towards the cave that had been hollowed into the ground. He could make out the door, an elaborate wooden structure blocking the entrance. "Wait." Carlos grabbed him by the arm and pulled him back. "You can't go in there."

"Well where are they then?"

"Patience, it's almost dusk." Carlos pointed toward the sun as it began to lower beneath the horizon, casting eerie shadows to haunt the clearing. They slumped onto a large rock and watched the sun set, waiting for nightfall.

As the last beams of light faded and twilight swallowed the land, Casper heard the wooden door's movement while it squeaked on old rusty hinges. He looked on in anticipation, trying to make out the cavern's entrance. Carlos fell to his knees as a figure emerged from the shadows, shrouded in dark robes.

"Oh cursed one, I have brought you a sacrifice. Its blood shall feed your people and wisdom shall flow forth from your lips into our minds." The figure looked down at Carlos as he addressed it. It reached out a hand, palm down, towards him. Raising it up, Carlos seemingly followed the motion and began floating skyward. After being lifted about a foot, he began spinning, starting slowly and speeding up. Out of control, he began yelling for help. Mystified by the actions, Casper stayed perfectly still, watching the mesmerizing body spin about. The hand slowly raised up higher as the figure pointed its palm towards Carlos. A scream radiated throughout the clearing as Casper noticed the man's skin peeling back off of his body, like a potato being deprived of its casing. The lifeless skin fell to the ground, leaving a grotesque mass of yelling organs behind. The shrouded creature raised its other hand and in response, the vital fluids of the body raised up into a ball. Directing with its hand, it moved the fluid from above Carlos' remains to a statue in the ground. Letting its hand fall to its side, the blood followed suit, dropping into a stone ball carved into the artwork. It then flicked its other wrist, causing the spinning organs to scatter about the clearing.

Casper let out a terrified gasp as the shrouded figure finally turned towards him. Jumping to his feet, he tore the machete from his belt and held it before him with both hands in a defensive manner.

"Come on, try that on me!" He yelled, trying to hide his terror.

"Foolish creature," the creature hissed in a sickeningly male voice. "That will do you no good." The creature's speech seemed to saturate the air around him, sending Casper into a nauseating euphoria. Without so much as a move from his opponent, Casper's machete was torn free from his white knuckles. Flying free through the air, it slid into a rock nearby so smoothly that it was as if it had cut through the rock like butter, despite the blade being weaker than the stone. He stared in awe at the sword as it quivered slightly and then stood still. The sound of a clearing throat reawakened Casper to the real world. Looking up, he saw the figure had moved back toward the door and was motioning towards it. "Come in, won't you?" It hissed. "We've been expecting you."

Casper looked at the door with apprehension before making his way cautiously to the cave entrance. His eyes never moved off of the floating figure as he passed it. The figure seemed to chuckle at his precautionary measures.

"I could end your life in a matter of seconds if I so choose to. Do not act as if I am your enemy. You have many things to fear, but do not make us one of them." It ended its remark with a stern hiss. Turning around, it followed Casper into the dark, damp cave. As he passed by sconces that lit the dim stairwell downwards, it showed to him various bones that had been scattered about on the stone steps.

"We have trouble entertaining guests." The creature behind him chuckled at its own dark joke, causing Casper to grimace at the thought of his own possible demise.

They arrived in a cavern lit by a strange glow emanating from the very rock walls. The center of the room consisted of a gigantically round stone table that came from the ground beneath it. Three more figures floated inside the cavern. Upon his arrival, they all turned to look at Casper. The tallest one, standing across the table from him, lifted its robes away from its head, causing Casper to gasp. The man's face was a paler white then he had ever seen, making his deep red lips stand out. The pale grey eyes made him feel uncomfortable as they peered darkly through him. Wisps of hair strayed about on his balding head. Pointed ears poked up towards the cavern's roof. Their eyes locked into a gaze and the creature breathed deeply in satisfaction. A grin spread across its face, letting fangs shine on the sickly red lips.

"Come, sit down," he cooed softly, "We have much to talk about." A long boney finger pointed to the table. "I am Nacafentu, leader of the Crosspien clan. Your mother told me you were coming." His grin widened with each word, giving Casper fear that he could barely control. Taking Nacafentu's offer, he walked to the table where a stone chair suddenly emerged from the ground. Looking slightly surprised, he sat in the new furniture and looked over the table toward the vampyre.

"Good," he hissed. "Let us start from the beginning, with your mother's murder."

Chapter 14

"Murder?" Casper jumped out of his chair and stared angrily at Nacafentu, seething with hatred.

"Calm down," Nacafentu's demeanor grew dark as he raised his hands up. Casper tried futilely to evade the motion only to find his body had become rigid and unresponsive through the vampyre's ancient magic. "What has been done cannot be changed. Do not blame us for the past."

"Well whose fault is it?" Casper growled, gaining control back of his facial muscles.

"Let's not be too hasty. First, I believe an offering is in order?" Casper shot a puzzling look at Nacafentu and then turned to the figure standing next to him, who had now removed its hood to reveal a face much like the first vampyre. "He was not your sacrifice, just your guide to come here." He replied, answering Casper's unasked question.

"Then why did you kill him?"

"He was no longer needed. His blood will provide a lovely feast for my clan." Casper had to think about Nacafentu's morbid answer for a minute.

"You told him to join Satan so he would eventually hunt me down." Casper accused. "You knew he'd bring me here." All the vampyres nodded in silent agreement. "But how did you know?"

"The future," Nacafentu answered firmly, "like all things, is merely knowledge, which we are masters of. Unfortunately for us, your future is clouded. You have more control over your destiny than any other. We knew you would come eventually, but we had to make sure you could find us." He pointed back towards Casper's original guide into the cavern who stood in silence. Casper turned back to give Nacafentu a puzzling look.

"So what do you want from me?"

"First we want your offering." He motioned to the other creatures and they started to surround him in a horrifying circle.

"To hell with that!" he exclaimed, leaping to his feet and assuming a defensive stance. Holding a palm face out, he let anger flow through his veins and into the hand. Flames danced on the surface of his hand, a warning for the vampyres to stay away.

"Don't be so naïve." Nacafentu heaved a short breath from across the room, causing the flames to sputter and send sparks about. Another shorter but harder breath extinguished the flame. "You don't even stand a chance. Now, all we ask is for your blood. An angel or demon holds bloodlines much stronger than any human's. They also form blood almost instantly so we do not kill them. Your heart pumps with both lines, so we ask for each of us to drink from your veins."

"If I refuse, what then, you'll kill me I suppose?"

"If you refuse, we will not need to kill you, lack of knowledge will be your undoing." Casper debated his choices and slowly lifted the tension on his body into submission. Closing his eyes, he could feel the first vampyre bend towards him. Hot breath washed over his neck, making the skin feel as if it was freezing instantly on its departure. His jaws hovered just inches from skin, enjoying the intoxicating sensations.

Finally content, the mouth bore down, letting sharp fangs slide into his neck. He winced in pain while blood flowed from his vein to the vampyre's mouth.

Finished with its feeding, the vampyre moved away to allow the next to step up. Searching with its tongue, its labored breaths stung at the bite marks already there.

"Delicious!" a delighted female voice hissed just before plunging her teeth into new puncture holes and drinking deeply from his neck. As she took her fill, Casper fell into a deep state of nauseating euphoria. Watching the room spin in a dim rotation, he could only barely feel the other two vampyres dig their fangs into him.

~~~~~~~~~~~~~~~~~~~~~~~~~~~~~~~~~

Casper awoke from his trance to see that all the vampyres had left the room save Nacafentu, who waited patiently against the wall on the other side of the table. Seeing that Casper was conscious, he walked to the table and summoned the stones into an elaborate throne next to him. He sat down promptly and turned to put an arm on Casper, causing him to shy away.

"Your mother..."

"What about my mother?" Casper asked, getting defensive. "What do you mean she was murdered? She fell in honorable battle. Wyburn told me himself." He looked into Nacafentu's eyes, which shifted towards the door. Moving to see what had caught his attention, he saw a familiar creature float in.

"I believe you've already met H'izveral." He said slowly. Casper looked back at him, wide eyed.

"No…" he moaned, shaking his head slowly. "Please don't." As he uttered his last words, a flash ignited the air around them.

The cavern faded into a brightly lit room. Marble pillars held up the ceiling as it arched high above. Angels scattered about with mythical creatures in a group gathered at the bottom of stairs carved into a golden hill. The top of the stairs was occupied by a throne, but they were so high up that Casper could barely make out who was sitting on it. He realized the light of the room was coming from atop the steps. He watched the scene sadly as he floated just above the silver tiles that made up the floor.

"Bring in the prisoner!" A voice boomed down from the throne, emanating throughout the hall and causing Casper to shake. The entire crowd bowed to one knee as the sound rained down upon them. He swam through the air to get closer for a better view.

"What's happening? Why'd you bring me here?" Casper began, looking back towards Nacafentu, who silenced him with a motion to continue watching. Turning back around, he saw two jailors carrying in a smaller, female figure. Only after they had thrown her onto the stairs and stepped away he could make out who it was. With a gasp, he pushed himself towards the beaten form of his mother. He tried to embrace her, but could only float by helplessly.

"You are but a visitor in this dream." Nacafentu said, still next to H'izveral. "You cannot change its outcome." Casper turned a burning glare back to Nacafentu, who shrugged empathically. "I'm sorry, truly I am."

"Aspriel, you have betrayed your rank and have made a mockery of us all!" The voice from the stairs once again thundered around them. Casper noticed out of the corner of his eye that the man on the throne had moved and was now walking down towards Aspriel. He squinted to get a better look only to realize that Zeus had been the one occupying the throne. As he walked regally down the golden stairs, Casper could start to make out more defining features of the mage. Short white hair accented his scalp and face. The mage was dressed in bright white robes that swept the staircase and seemed to move gracefully in one continuous movement. Scars ran down his arms and up into the sleeveless robes. They resembled lighting bolts, making Casper wonder what had truly caused them. He was truly a frightening sight altogether.

"You killed a surrendering general, High treason in our laws." He descended until he stood halfway down the stairs to Aspriel. Raising one hand high into the air, he lifted her from where she had fallen and made her float up the staircase. He dropped his hand to make her fall into a bundle at his feet, where she looked up with anger masking her fear. "How do you plead?"

"I killed the leading general for…"

"I asked how you plead!"

"This was Dafierno, the…"

"Do not make me repeat myself again!" Zeus' voice roared in impatient rage. "I want none of your excuses. How do you plead?"

"G-guilty," she stuttered quietly, looking down.

"And you know the punishment for your crime?" Aspriel nodded her lowered head. Zeus motioned towards the crowd. "Then we shall proceed. We will have your successor come forward!" A figure walked slowly from the crowd, head bowed. Shocked, Casper could only watch the figure as he passed by him at the base of the stairs.

"Wyburn, do no try to prolong the inevitable. You know what must happen!" The slightly younger Wyburn looked up and quickened his pace only slightly as he climbed the stairs, stopping next to Aspriel's bowed figure. "Bring forth Yungfel!" As Zeus' words echoed throughout the arched room, one of Aspriel's jailors carried her claymore up to where the three figures were standing. Bowing, he presented the sword to Wyburn, who took it painfully from him. The jailor rose from his bow and hurried down the stairs. Wyburn turned painfully back to Zeus, holding the claymore at ready.

The claymore drew blood from Wyburn's wrist as he drew it across his skin and bit back a painful cry. He let the blade soak fully in his blood before looking back up to Zeus.

"I am ready."

"Then commence!" Zeus commanded, lifting his hands up high. Wyburn turned toward Aspriel, lowering the sword to her face.

"I'm sorry, my love…" he whispered through the tears on his face.

"No!" Casper yelled, turning his face away as Wyburn swung the sword towards her neck. He heard the sword make contact as everyone winced at the execution.

"It is done! She has paid for her crimes!" Weeping uncontrollably, he brought himself to look up at Zeus' remark. Wyburn dropped the sword soundly onto the steps, where it slid lazily down towards Casper. Dropping to his knees, Wyburn embraced Aspriel's headless body. Zeus ascended back up the stairs towards his throne, leaving Wyburn to cry into Aspriel's still form. Casper shuddered with despair. Unable to accept the fate, he looked on in disbelief with pain stricken eyes. As Wyburn sobbed into the lifeless body, a soft glow floated out of Aspriel and up towards the ceiling, to where a past form of H'izveral hovered above. It shrieked silently as it collected another soul and faded back into vaporous air.

"We must now deal with the cyspherion. You know your duties," Zeus proclaimed as he sat smugly on his throne. "Because of him, our portal to earth is restricted. Wyburn, you shall be responsible for taking care of this. Do not return until you have done so." Wyburn did nothing to acknowledge Zeus, only rock softly with Aspriel's body.

The room faded into a dark light as the cavern reappeared around them. Casper, hunched over, cried in the corner as H'izveral turned to Nacafentu, who nodded to approve dismissal. It floated slowly towards the door, disappearing without a trace of ever having been there.

"He killed her." Casper said through tears. "She died at the hands of her own husband."

"I know. I'm sorry, I truly am. Everyone has a choice. He chose loyalty over love."

"But h-how? He killed my mother just to keep position with Zeus? What about true love?"

"We have decisions and he felt that this was the best choice. Be thankful he did not follow through and kill you." Casper looked back up in total confusion.

"Even the forces of good would kill me just to open the Wrokthien Portals?"

"Once again, Wyburn failed to inform you on all of the details. The portals were a mere inconvenience compared to what they were really after. You were created by GOD as an abnormality. What happened between your mother and father should have never come to pass. Due to your unstable nature he had to safeguard your powers until you were old enough to learn how to control them. Because of this, your magic stood untouched and clean within. If an alignment could obtain this power before you became old enough, it would give incredible powers to their cause. Unfortunately the only way they could tap into your powers would be to destroy you. Wyburn, being what Zeus considered to be your true father, charged him with the task of killing you. For the past twenty one years he has been out to destroy the cyspherion. The first time he laid eyes on you however, he knew instantly who you were. He followed you for twelve years afterwards, waiting for the chance to assassinate you. Always the shadow you could feel but never see. Without Zeus to command him, he could never bring himself to kill the last piece of Aspriel he had left. Although he did come close in the church the day before your birthday, he still could never do it." Melancholy turned to rage in Casper's eyes as he listened to Nacafentu.

"You mean this whole time he's wanted to kill me?" Casper yelled. "I listened to an assassin?" He grabbed the table in attempts to flip it, but it stayed embedded in the ground and only served to anger him further. He shot a fireball at it in defeat, leaving a black scorch mark across its surface.

"But he didn't," Nacafentu stated, grabbing Casper's hands and pinning them down before he lit another fireball and cause more damage. "He chose to let you live, though he defied his leader's wishes and may lose his position and even his life over it." Casper struggled against the vampyre's embrace, but couldn't compete against the old creature's strength. He settled down after tiring himself out.

"You must go on to find your path. It will be a tough decision, but when it comes down to the choice, follow when you know in your heart to be right." Casper let Nacafentu's words sink in as he slid out of his arms.

"So I should go back to Heresen?"

"Not yet. You only have basic knowledge of your powers. You need a mentor to learn from. Conventionally, this would be done by your parents. As you can guess, this is impossible for you. Luck will still strike for you, though. There is a mercenary of war eighty miles west of here. He inhabits a smoldering volcano where he lives in solitude, taking on any contracts between Heaven and Hell that pay right. He knows the forces of good and evil well and can teach you how to use them."

"But how…"

"Do you pay him?" the vampyre finished Casper's sentence. "Just tell him Nacafentu sent you. We have a contract he has yet to pay for and teaching you should prove sufficient in relinquishing his debt."

"How do I find him?"

"He will allow you to find him, just let the smoke guide you." He moved his hand above the table, causing a transparent vision of a volcano to appear over it, surrounded by the jungle. Smoke flowed out of the top of it and sunk down into the jungle, creating paths to aid in the search of it. "His name is Jasselbad and he is a fallen angel." Nacafentu retracted his hand and as quickly as the volcano appeared, it vanished.

"I'll get there as quickly as possible." Casper promised, starting to turn.

"Wait," Nacafentu grabbed his wrist before he could walk away. "Aren't you forgetting something?" He raised his eyebrow and stared inquisitively at the confused man. They shared the stare for what seemed like too long.

"How about this?" The vampyre finally asked, waving his hand back over the table. The volcano vanished instantly and in its stead was Harbieno. Casper scarcely recognized the part of town that was being shown to him. Traveling through the small town, the vision chose a poorly built building and entered the door. On the other side he could see creatures standing around two figures in chairs. As the vision closed in, Casper could make out the faces.

"Poncho, Isabella!" He gasped at the two Mexicans tied to chairs, guarded closely by Demonic followers. "I know exactly where that is," He grunted, pulling his hand away from Nacafentu and running out of the doorway and up the stairwell.

"Good," Nacafentu whispered to the disappearing figure. "You have done well Casper and I know you will choose the right path. I just know you will, I can feel it in your heart."

Meanwhile above ground, Casper reached the surface and burst into the dark clearing. He stopped only momentarily to pull the machete free of its home in the stone before running to free his two young friends. Even without knowledge of the area, he ran blindly forward to where he thought the village was. It would seem that he was being directed to Harbieno by an unforeseen force.

Chapter 15

The room was filled with darkness, making it impossible for Poncho to see who his captors were. He and Isabella were knocked unconscious only moments after Casper had left them in the café. They came to in the lightless room with odd creatures all about. He could hear them growling and talking but couldn't recognize their voices. Reaching over as best he could, he found that Isabella was tied next to him. Wrapping his hand around her delicate fingers, he felt her as she squeezed his hand tightly, a slight comfort for both of them. The dirty rag serving as a gag gave off a disgusting taste as he tried to work it out of his mouth.

"Where is he?" A creature nearby hissed. "He should have been back here hours ago. All he had to do was kill the cyspherion and bring his body back."

"Maybe he brought him back to Satan himself, you know, take all the credit alone?"

"Shut up, Carlos wouldn't do that to us!" a female voice yelled.

"Just because you're infatuated with him doesn't mean he won't sell us short!" Anger flared throughout the room, making Poncho feel very uncomfortable. The rage filled words became jumbled as each one started talking over the other.

"Wait!" One voice screamed over the others as he slammed his hand against a hard surface, probably a table Poncho guessed. "What about his two little spies?"

"What of them?"

"What're we going to do with them anyway?"

"Well I've got an idea for the girl anyway." Poncho heard the man chuckling gleefully as he approached Isabella. She shrieked and flailed helplessly as an unclean hand groped her leg. Finally able to manipulate the gag from his mouth, Poncho pushed it down to rest around his neck.

"You guys don't stand a chance!" He yelled. "Casper's gonna come and kick your ass!" A hand flew through the air, slapping hard against his face and forcing it to one side.

"Shut up, no one told you to talk." Poncho bit his lip to conceal the pain as the man spit at him. "So you think your friend's going to come save you? Let me tell you something little boy. Carlos is the best assassin we have in this village, he won't fail us. Your friend's as good as dead." Although dark in the room, Poncho could see the man sneering just inches from his body as his breath blew into his face, forcing the ghastly scent of rotten meat into his nostrils.

"I watched him kill a cougar with only a machete. He can take your friend!" Poncho accented the yell with spit, hitting his mark directly in front of him. The man ruthlessly slapped Poncho's unprotected face again.

"Well Carlos would've killed it barehanded." The nauseating voice shot back as he raised his hand for another hit. A foreign sound made him stop to listen intently. "What was that noise?" He asked, pausing in mid strike.

"Someone's at the door."

"Well, go see who it is." The creature walked cautiously toward the front doorway, creeping on the ground like a wolf.

He reached up slowly for the handle only moments before the door came crashing down off of its hinges, trapping the creature underneath.

Moonlight flooded into the room, showing to the rest of its occupants Casper's figure with his leg extended from the kick as his eyes glowed a deathly red. He lowered his leg slowly, looking around with indifference, face frozen in a scowl.

"Get him!" Someone yelled from the back of the room, breaking the momentary silence. Casper instantly jumped into the room, landing on the door to crush the body underneath. Sounds of crunching came from the trapped man as a few of the people transformed into wolves, growling at the cyspherion who stood unmoving from his stance on top of the door. From what Casper could seem there were three therions, two humans, and one minor demon and in the center, Poncho and Isabella. The closest therion lunged for him, teeth bearing and claws extended. Side stepping off of the wooden door, he slid the machete out from his belt and slashed at the leaping figure, catching it off guard. Whimpering in anger, the therion landed nearby as Casper, who had not stopped but instead continued his attack by spinning to slash at a nearby woman's throat. She fell to the ground with a thud, blood gushing from a gaping hole in her neck. The wounded therion got back up to its feet atop the broken door, growling as he prepared for another attack. Whirling around, Casper lit flames on his fingers and whipped them down at the wooden door, igniting it instantly in flames. The creature yelped as his fur caught fire. A flaming ball of light ran out of the doorway and down the street as he tried desperately to extinguish the burning coat of fur. Underneath the burning wood, a scream let out as the dying man realized he was now trapped by a fiery door.

Turning back to the other opponents, Casper raised his bloody sword above head level and smirked. Twisting his wrists around in a circle, he took two steps forward and let the blade fly towards the minor demon, who grabbed the blade in mid-flight with its clawed hands. He grunted with evil glee while easily trying to force the machete away from his head. Losing the battle of strength, Casper tried a new tactic. Leaning his weight forward, he pushed against the demon's arms with the sword until he was sure that all of his strength was pushing against the demon. With a quick action, he let go with his left hand. Letting the demon pass by, Casper dived into a forward roll along his right side as the demon stumbled forward, no longer having an opponent to contend with. As Casper rolled by, he slid the machete away from the demon's claws, slicing its thick hands as it passed. He sprung to his feet and spun around. Digging the machete deep into its back, Casper felt the demon retch as the blade sliced all the way through his chest cavity. The cold metal in its chest caused it to shriek in pain before falling face down into the ground, sliding lifelessly off the blade.

Giving his attention to the captives, Casper ran to them and swiftly cut the ropes binding them to the seats.

"We've got to get out of here!" he barked, spinning to search for any close threats. Two therions had closed in and were ready to attack. Leaping in unison, they flew towards them as a double threat. Casper turned his machete sideways and spun around in a giant circle, using the outstretched blade as an aggressive shield. Unprotected stomachs of the therions were sliced through as they reached his metallic arc. It took only a moment for them to regain their footing and they turned their noses towards the roof in preparation to howl.

"Damn," He muttered under his breath.

"What?" Poncho had stood up just behind him and now looked over his shoulder. Not bothering to answer his question, he hastily aimed for their snouts and lobbed off both of their jaws before they got a chance to make a sound.

"They were going to call for their hell hound pack." He answered, turning back to Poncho as he spoke. "Don't worry, I stopped them." The three of them looked back to see the two therions writhing in pain as they transformed back to the human form. The change however, did not serve to help them but cause them even more intense pain. Their lower jaw and nose were missing and only bloody flaps of flesh hung loosely on their facial features.

"We need to get out of here." Casper said. "Before..." a dagger slipped around Casper's neck, cutting his sentence off as the last human stood behind him. Forgotten until this point, he had taken the moment to ambush Casper.

"Surprise!" He yelled. "Satan's going to love this." Casper could feel the dagger slowly pressing against his skin and slowly moved his hand with the machete, trying to get a clear shot at the body behind him.

"I don't think so." The man sneered, grabbing the machete and throwing it carelessly to the side. Casper felt him tighten his grip on his neck and thought desperately. An idea came to him and quickly reached down, trying not to be noticed.

"Wait." He grunted. "Won't you grant me one last request?" He slowly slid his hand around the grip of Carlos' gun, which had remained holstered unnoticed there until this point.

"I guess I can grant you one last request. What is it? Make it quick." The human huffed as he loosened the tight grip he had on the cyspherion, giving him just a little more room. "I haven't got all day."

"Die!" Casper yelled while pulling the gun from his belt and pointing it over his shoulder. Squeezing the trigger as fast as possible, he let three bullets fly into the man's face and felt warm blood splash against his skin. The man slowly fell to the ground, gurgling with pain. Casper brushed himself off promptly before turning to pry the dagger from his cold hands. As he stepped away from the body, he bent down to pick up the machete from the ground.

"Well?" he said nonchalantly towards Poncho and Isabella. "Are we going to get out of here or wait for their friends to show up?" He tossed the dagger lightly to Poncho and turned to walk towards the smoldering door. The short lived flames had exhausted its fuel supply too quickly and now all that remained was charred embers scattered around a burnt skeleton. Stepping to the side, Casper let the two of them exit the building first, watching them dance carefully around the bones. Shrugging, he followed close behind, giving the skull a firm kick on his way by and watching it with contentment as the blackened bone slammed against the doorjamb and bounced outside, rolling off into a bush.

"Where are we going?" Poncho asked once they had all assembled in the dark street. "I think people are going to notice us now." He pointed out by motioning to the house behind them.

"We, my friend, are going to pay a visit to Jasselbad," he remarked with a smirk, starting his walk down the road. Turning slightly to see if they were following, he caught sight of a fiery object approaching quickly. The flaming therion that had run out earlier was now approaching them at an alarming rate. Even more aflame then before, they watched as he passed them by in full run, howling with all of his might.

"Who's Jasselbad?" Poncho asked, ignoring the burning wolf form and turning back to Casper.

"Hope you knew who he was…" he said. "No Harbieno myths about a fallen angel?" Poncho stopped and turned to speak with Isabella, who stayed silent in thought.

"No, we've never heard of Jasselbad." Poncho translated from Isabella as she sighed in Spanish. "But we'll be more than happy to help you find him." He tucked the dagger firmly into his pants. Not having a belt himself, he had to settle for using his bare jeans to hold the weapon.

They started walking towards the jungle's edge while the fading sounds of a howling therion, desperate to find refuge from the flames, slowly faded out until he had either ran out of earshot or more likely burned to death.

"How many more of those deviants you think live around Harbieno?" Casper asked as he kept his focus on the green trees ahead.

"Hard to tell, it was dark, they look like any kind of human to me."

"They mark themselves with a pentagram most likely done in pen, on their wrists. That's how they show their loyalty to Satan."

"And your marks mean you with GOD?" Poncho asked, indicating the crosses on his wrists.

"These," He growled, stopping to turn around and confront Poncho by holding his wrists up for the both of them to see. "Were branded on me against my will. I think I was born with them but still, I am aligned with no one and will answer to no one." The markings seemed to glow a dull red in response to the anger in Casper's angry tone, making it easier for them to see him in the dim moonlight. "All I care about is avenging my mother." He finished and turned to walk further, leading them onward and into the jungle's edge.

Reaching the tree line, Casper stopped and turned to look at the two Mexican children trailing behind him. Giving them both a stern look, he held up one hand in a motion for them to stop.

"Its dangerous out there, you both know that. I don't want to be responsible for anything that happens to her," he pointed to Isabella. "It would probably be best for you to stay here in the protection of the village."

"No! I lost her once already and I'm not about to part with her again." Poncho reached out and forced Casper's reluctant hand to his side. "What if more of the creatures come to the village and find out what happened and what you did there? She be safer with us. She come with us and that's final." Isabella stared at him with a puzzling look as he stood defiantly against Casper. Turning to address her, Poncho spoke once again in rapid Spanish, explaining the situation while she nodded in somber agreement.

"Fine," Casper said in defeat, gazing back into to the jungle. "I wouldn't want to have to save you again anyway. You guys are more of a pain then you're worth." He led them a few feet into the jungle as he spoke. "Just do me a favor and teach her some English so I can communicate with the damn girl."

"Alright, you got a deal." Poncho grinned in triumph. Taking Isabella's hand in his own, they followed Casper into the dark wilderness.

"And one more thing," Casper said sternly, pausing in his tracks. "You protect your own girlfriend. She's not my problem and I'm not risking my life on her."

"You got it," Poncho said with just a little less enthusiasm. The walk continued forward, stepping through the thick plant life. The plants gripped their clothes as they tried to pick their way through the dense branches. With an exasperated sigh, Casper pulled his machete free and began to hack a path through the impassable fauna.

"How we going to find him anyway? You know where you going?" Poncho asked after a while of silence.

"We're looking for a trail of smoke. It'll lead us to him." It suddenly occurred to him that he had been walking blindly instead of looking for the volcano's path. Poncho translated to Isabella and looking down simultaneously, the three began searching the ground for any trace amounts of smoke.

"I'm surprised you even believe anything you've seen so far." Casper stated after a moment, still looking down at the ground. "Don't you find it hard to believe that Satan's followers just kidnapped you and you were almost killed by a demon and a pack of therions?" Poncho shook his head in silence, still searching for the path. "Further more, I tell you we're going to be brought to a fallen angel by way of smoke, yet you follow me and help me look?" Poncho tried to hide the grin from his face only to fail miserably.

"I always thought maybe there was more to the world then what they tell us." He said slyly. "It's exciting to find out that all the myths are real." Casper looked up to eye the boy. "Haven't you ever dreamed of being a wizard or something magical?" He asked, looking up to meet Casper's gaze. Casper shook his head before returning his focus back down to the ground. A shriek sounded off just a few feet away from them, making them both jump.

"Isabella!" Poncho shouted in panic as they ran toward the sound. They were met with the unexpected sight of her dancing excitedly around, shouting something in Spanish and pointing to the earth. They looked down to see a puff of smoke billowing about near a tree root and connecting to a trail leading deeper into the untamed wilds.

"Let's go!" Casper shouted in excitement, running towards the source of the smoke, slashing madly about with his sword, making a rushed and ragged path.

"Alright, someone in a hurry." Poncho yelled, grabbing Isabella's hand and rushing through the roughly cut trail. "Slow down a little or we going to lose you."

"Sorry," he called back, not bothering to slow down. "Jasselbad's at the end of the trail. I need him to teach me all of his fighting skills. My mother was murdered before I even met her. Her killer will not go unpunished! I will avenge her death!" He ran onwards, barely even bothering to cut as he went. Hot on the trail, the smoke motivated him onwards and his adrenaline masked the pain as each branch whipped his body in passing.

Poncho apologized repeatedly to Isabella as he dragged her through the jungle, trying as hard as possible not to lose Casper into the dark horrors of the night.

Unnoticed by the three friends glared a pair of bright eyes, following not far behind. Glinting in the moonlight, they slid in and out of the jungle's obstacles with practiced ease. Keeping up with them was not a problem for him and he licked his lips in anticipation as the chase continued. The jungle would wear them out long before he would tire. He had the time to wait. Vengeance pushed forward harder then hunger. The hunter knew this chase would not end well for his prey.

Chapter 16

Tired eyes strained to keep their sights on the smoke. They had been traveling countless hours and still no goal was in sight. Fatigue had slowed them considerably and they now only stumbled through the jungle, barely able to even keep their balance.

"Alright, we need to take a break." Casper huffed as he stumbled to his knees. Even for him, the quest for Jasselbad was becoming strenuous and tiring. Poncho and Isabella followed in suit, falling onto the ground while panting from the rigorous hike. "We'll continue on in a couple of minutes." He huffed, closing his eyes and leaning against a tree.

"This smoke's going on forever." Poncho complained as Isabella leaned against him, using his stomach as a pillow. He looked down, soothing her with words while brushing his hand through her tangled hair. Sweat poured down their bodies, staining their clothing and making them feel extremely unclean. Grunting, Casper exerted himself by pulling at his shirt to rip it apart down the middle and letting it hang like a vest. Feeling slightly cooler, he slumped back and sighed in exhaustion.

The sun overhead stung their eyes and made it harder to see the smoky trail. They had to backtrack several times just to stay on the path.

"Maybe we should wait till nightfall." Poncho sighed, still trying to control his breathing. "The smoke seems to show up better in night." Casper turned to him and nodded in approval.

"I think you're right, this smoke is almost impossible to see during the day." Rolling his head against the tree, he sighed and started slipping into a light sleep. Nearby, their pursuer slowed down to a halt, easily staying hidden in the shadows. He grinned wickedly in anticipation. They were tired and would soon be asleep, making themselves easy targets. He glared intently through the underbrush but was not satisfied with his vantage point. He leapt effortlessly to the branches above to hold the higher ground. The one who had hurt him was sleeping, but the other two were still awake. He wanted to take no chances, so watched from above as the boy and girl talked in a strange tongue, happy to be together. It was a waiting game, but he had all the time in the world and revenge kept him alert.

● ~~~~~~~~~~~~~ ● ~~~~~~~~~~~~~~ ●

"Maverick...Maverick, listen to me." Casper awoke to hear a gruff voice calling his last name. The voice was so deep and disheartening that it was as if the pits of Hell were calling him. Squinting through blinking eyes, Casper saw the area about him start to clear. Surrounded by a reddish yellow light, it would seem that it was all the world was made up of. Illusions of the jungle fought through the darkly yellow glow, becoming transparent apparitions. He looked over only to see Poncho and Isabella speaking sweetly to each other. Leaning over, he tried standing by pushing against a tree, only to have his hand pass right through.

"Wha-what's going on here?" Casper asked. Stunned by the surreal world, he stumbled to his feet and looked all about him. "What happened to the jungle? Am I dead?" he yelled to the estranged jungle.

"Calm down, you are not dead." The evil voice growled. "You are consciously asleep. I need to speak with you." Casper turned instinctively around to confront the voice. Craning his head upwards, he recognized the nine foot behemoth before him.

"Father?" Casper questioned in awe, looking with confusion at the vision of Dafierno standing right in front of him.

"Yes my child. I have been unable to contact you until now. I've been denied message to my own son through protection of Zeus' soldiers. Now that you lie out here alone with just these two children, I was able to tap into your unprotected dreams."

"But how? I needed Aspriel's blood to contact her."

"You are right my son, but your body was formed out of my blood. Therefore you can use it to talk to me." He bent down on one knee, bringing his face close to Casper's. "I once thought killing was my only purpose in life. I now know that life has many opportunities and reasons." Dafierno's lips curled over his fangs when he talked, letting saliva slide out of his mouth. "Your mother taught me that, even if she didn't realize it," he continued, putting his clawed hand on Casper's hair and stroking it down behind his head. "I only wish she would not have killed me in the process. For over eight hundred years I had taken orders but on that battlefield, in full sight of her, I wanted to defy Satan and deny my alignment."

"Then why didn't you then? You just couldn't?"

"Well at least not without my head." He chuckled. "If I hadn't been killed, I could have perhaps dejected and lived in exile. Even though I wouldn't have been with Aspriel, I could have at least traded my damned path for a more enlightened one. None of this matters though. Without my death you would not exist, so my death was not in vain. My son, you carry the torch of hope for everyone."

"What do you want from me? I'm no hero. I didn't even know my real parents until now."

"I apologize, but I could not see you until the war within you had subsided. Now that your alignment is equalizing, you have the power to talk to Aspriel and myself. You truly can be a hero, for a balance of good and evil flows through you. Not only can you feel the pull of both sides but you can distinguish it in the world. Not one side can be appropriate for every situation. Good must be used just as much as evil to maintain overall peace."

"I think you mean evil should be used as equally as good?" Dafierno raised one eyebrow as he stared back at him. "Sorry," he apologized, remembering that it was a nether demon he was speaking to. "You may be right, but what do you care of the preservation of Earth? You're a nether demon that has been killed in battle. What right do you have here?"

"You are my son," Dafierno stated strongly as he wrapped his monstrous hands around Casper's incredibly smaller arms. Staring down at the giant arms that held him, Casper could see the intricate markings of a pentagram surrounding by fire. Inside it was the name Dafierno, as fiery as the sun. "Even though I am a nether demon, I can still love my son. I wish to see you succeed in your quest."

"And what is my quest?"

"You must bring peace between the forces and create a balance point to tether it to. Only then will this pointless war cease."

"All I want to do is kill Wyburn. If I solve world peace in the process, then so be it."

"I know you hate him," Dafierno tightened his grip on Casper's arms, making him wince. "Do you think that I myself like that beast of an animal? He married and executed the one woman I could have loved. Revenge will bring you nothing but woe. You need to concentrate on what is important. Perhaps Wyburn can even help you fulfill your destiny. As heartless and incompetent as he may be, he was also assigned as your assassin. If he could betray Zeus to keep you alive, he may just prove to be a worthy ally." The two locked gazes. It was the closest to a father and son moment either one had witnessed.

"But I don't even know where to start." Casper said as the feeling quickly grew uncomfortable. He quickly pulled himself away from Dafierno while trying to return to his tough attitude. "How am I suppose to save the world?"

"You are on the right path," he answered with a chuckle. "Go to Jasselbad. He will teach you the proper way to fight. Though you quest for peace, bloodshed will still be in your future." He glanced over to Poncho and Isabella. "They're falling asleep," he said as Casper followed the gaze. "You three are no longer safe here!" Dafierno's eyes snapped back to Casper. "I must let you go for now my son, but I will see you soon."

"Wait, what do you mean?"

"You are about to be attacked. A predator hides in waiting for them to fall sleep. Wake up and defend yourself!" The jungle started shimmering back into reality as he felt the waking shadows on his eyes. "Fight back with your eternal fire, let its bitter dance engulf you and be forever lost in its rapturous soul." They were the final words Casper heard from Dafierno as he was thrown violently back against the tree he had fallen asleep against.

Jumping to his feet, he shook the strange dream from his eyes just in time to see the incoming predator looking for blood. Leaping lightly to the side, he let the incoming creature collide uncontrollably with the tree trunk. The sound of impact woke Poncho and Isabella instantly.

"What the hell? These woods infested with cougars?" Poncho yelled, stepping forward to protect Isabella while pulling his dagger free. Meanwhile, Casper had already readied his machete and pointed toward the stunned cat.

"I don't think so," He replied, walking in a slow circle around it. "Look at his shoulder!" Poncho looked to where he was pointing and gasped at the sight of a giant gash running through its body. "That's the same cougar? But how? You killed it."

"How should I know? Its like the damn cat spawned from Hell or something." Casper back away slightly as the cougar shook the daze from his head and spun to growl angrily at him. "I already killed you once damn it. What's your problem?" The only answer he received was a vicious hiss as the large feline pushed off the ground towards Casper in a deadly attack. As he watched it pass by, Poncho gripped the dagger hard in his hand and stuck it out in cat's path. It found a home in his furry flesh as the dagger's blade ripped skin apart, giving the cougar another deep slash across his opposite side. Unable to stop himself in mid flight, the cat took the painful cut, falling once again to the ground. Not giving him a second to regain his ground, Poncho kicked the cougar's side, making it roll over. With all of his might, he drove the dagger deep into the unprotected heart, letting a growl escape his lips.

"Let's see you come back to life now!" He yelled to the wriggling beast as it yowled in pain. With a satisfied grunt, Poncho looked back up to Casper. "I don't think he be giving us any problem now." He pulled himself up off of the carcass only after the creature had stopped moving. Blood dripped from the knife's tip as he held it by his side. Isabella ran proudly to her boyfriend, giving him a hug and shouting what Casper assumed was praise.

"Thank you," he mumbled, surprised that his life had just been saved by a fifteen year old boy. "I think we should move on. I don't know what's going on here, but we're not going to be safe until we find shelter."

They picked themselves up and started through the dense surroundings, keeping their guards up for any other attacks. The first encounter was too close of a call and a second one could be devastating.

Twigs snapped and smaller animals ran for cover, rushing to evacuate the path Casper was making. The smoke curled around his feet, as if to pull him forwards to its hidden destination. He ignored the encroaching smoke as every footstep brought back the words of his father. Since he had met Nacafentu revenge clouded his mind, but after talking to his father, thoughts of allying with Wyburn shuddered through his body. The lesser angel was crazy, at least in Casper's mind. He couldn't begin to believe that the only way to save the world would be to befriend him.

"Look!" The sound of Poncho's yell shook the daydreams from him. His finger pointed to a great volcano looming not far in front of them. Smoke rose regally from its mouth in such a beautiful pattern that Casper could only stare in disbelief. The grey cloud created by the venting smoke slowly dissipated down to the jungle earth, letting its tendrils flow through the tree trunks. He quickly realized it was the source of his path and began to run vigorously towards terrifyingly gorgeous monstrosity. Smoke thickened around his body as he pushed through each branch, hardly even bothering with the machete as he ran on. Ash began to collect on his body while the nearby wildlife began showing signs of death.

As he approached the base of the volcano, blight seemed to poison the ground around him.

He could hear Poncho and Isabella's distant sounds of struggle as they tried their best to keep up. Uncaring, he sped forward, letting the gap between them grow. They would be able to find him once he met Jasselbad.

Skidding to a stop at the base, he gazed around the mountain, searching for any openings or doorways. Entry through the vent itself would be almost impossible as it was filled with smoke and undoubtedly would be holding magma within. Not seeing a visible entrance made him sigh in irritation, letting Isabella and Poncho catch up to him.

"Spread out," He ordered as they raced to his side. "Look for any doorway or cave that someone could live in." Poncho relayed the message to his girlfriend, who nodded with approval. Spreading out in different directions, they started combing the desolate volcano side. Aside from a few rocks and burnt grass, they came up empty handed. There was no apparent way to enter the volcano, which only furthered to anger the tired trio. They had been hiking through the deadly jungle only to come to the desolate location with no answers.

Furrowing his brow in frustration, Casper threw one of the collected rocks towards the volcano's mouth.

"Where are you, Jasselbad?" He yelled to the heavens. "Where is your secret hiding place?"

"Smoke clears your vision as you answer my sacrificial decision!" A booming voice echoed across the ground. The three friends stood atop the volcano side, astounded by the sudden voice. Each one glanced at another with a perplexing look on their face.

"What the hell does that mean?" Casper asked after a moment of silent confusion.

"Oh ta 'ell with it, juss' come ta tha edge ov tha volcano's mouth!" It yelled back. Shrugging his shoulders, Casper led the two teenagers toward the top of the mountain. With their bare hands shielding themselves from the heat, they forged slowly onward. As they reached the edge, the smoke slowly cleared away from an illuminated area. Magma lit up a staircase etched into the rock. Casper smiled in satisfaction as they linked hands and began the treacherous descent down the small, slippery steps. A door came hazily into view as they walked on. It seemed to be worked from some kind of strange steel, much like the dagger that had been used to murder Alyssa. Casper promptly decided it to be not a material from this world. He approached the door, making sure to keep his footing and pressed his palm firmly against it. To his surprise, even the dangerously high temperatures of the volcano could not warm the metal and the door stayed cool and moist to the touch. Pushing it with great force, he pressed his weight against it. The door stayed firm, not even moving an inch. The harder he pushed, the more it seemed to stay in place.

"Pull et, stupid." The voice thundered in aggravation. Glancing down, Casper suddenly became aware that a bar was jutting out from the door's middle. Colored the same bright grey as the door, he had easily overlooked it. Gripping it with one hand, he budged it open and stumbled inside, pulling the chain of humans along with him.

As the door closed behind them, it took with it a large gust of wind. The air about them grew instantly cooler. They rose to their feet as they confronted a silhouetted figure.

"Why 'ello loves." Jasselbad said grinning while he held a menacing axe at ready.

Chapter 17

Casper, Isabella and Poncho stared in fascination at the creature before them. Loosely resembling an angel, Jasselbad stood around five and a half feet tall. Although short, he made up for it with bulging muscles, threatening to rip through his tight and shining flesh. His bald head reflected the torchlight except for one deep scar, running from the back of his neck over the top of his head to the side of his mouth, passing straight through his right eye socket which was concealed by a greasy black patch. A chain mail vest hung from his broad shoulders. On closer inspection, Casper noted that the rings were in a dragonscale weave, a very rare and protective design. The metal looked to be made out of a mysteriously strong metal, far better then steel. The angel's knuckles were wrapped in brown leather gauntlets cut off at the fingers. His massive hands seemed dangerous enough alone to produce collateral damage, but still held a strangely recognizable battle axe. His legs stood shoulder length apart and were shrouded in thick leathery armor that tucked into large, black boots. Wings folded out from his back, darker then the night but dotted with shining feathers of silver.

"Ah, neva seen a fallen angel before, have yer, mates?" Jasselbad sneered. The three friends could only shake their heads, keeping their eyes glued to him. "Well ya better start a talkin' lessen ya enjoy bleedin' on my ground, eh? Now who ar ya an why ya tresspassin' on ma property?" Jasselbad's accent reminded Casper of a Scottish pirate, which intrigued him. If he had not felt that his life was on the line, he would most likely have laughed at the strange speech pattern. Jasselbad stared at them, still waiting for a response. When none came, he shifted the weight of his weapon over, drawing it back to prepare a strike.

"Wait!" Casper yelled, finally able to find his voice. "I'm Casper, Nacafentu sent me to find you. These are my friends."

"Er, now why wood tha ole' bat send a wee little shrimp loik yerself?"

"I'm the cyspherion. I'm here to learn how to fight from you." Casper shot back defensively, standing up as he spoke.

"Tha cyspherion eh? I woulda espected somethin' bigga, love. Alrioght, prove yer tha legundairy cyspherion an not sum useluss punk." Casper flipped his wrists around, revealing the tattoos that haunted his skin.

"How's that do it for you?" Casper raised his eyebrow as Jasselbad studied the marks closely.

"So ya got tha markings? Well that'll do it fer me. So I guess tha axe is rightfully yers then eh? It belonged to ya fatha." He paused to run his hand affectionately down the hefty axe handle, signaling that he adored the weapon. "But I've a gotten so attached ta it durin' tha years. And I dun think it suits ya." He grinned maliciously as he put his evil gaze back on Casper.

"Yeah, you keep it," Casper replied quickly, "I'm more of a sword man myself."

"Excellent choice thar my friend, Come on now, I'll be a showin ya my home." Jasselbad turned and beckoned them to follow.

"So you deserted Zeus' cause?" Casper asked as the three of them ran to keep up.

"Now Why ya be sayin' that, matey?" Jasselbad turned and glared at him. "Ya insinuatin' that I'm a bad guy then, huh? I'll 'ave ya know I haven't deserted my cause once in ma life."

"I just thought that since you're a fallen angel..." Casper said, trying to save himself before Jasselbad interrupted his stuttering speech.

"I be a fallun angel, aye. That mean I be in tha neutral cause. Didn' Nacafentu explain that to ya?" Jasselbad extended his arm, showing strange markings across his wrists. Gazing closely, Casper examined the new artwork with interest. The alignment symbol depicted a pillar leaning slightly to the left. Vines wrapped around its midsection while sideways eights adorned the top and bottom of each pillar. Casper instantly recognized the pillar as it closely resembled the letter I in the name Michael from his own wrists. On both sides stood sideway crowns made up of three spikes extending outwards. Jasselbad's name appeared in the symbol as Casper had come to suspect.

"That's the neutral symbol?" Casper asked in surprise.

"Well it ain't cheese strudels that's fer sure." Jasselbad looked up to see Casper's puzzled face as he looked on with Poncho and Isabella. "Ya neva seen thes, have ya loves? Now dun tell me Nacafentu neva showed ya his wrists? Damn it boy, it looks like ya got a lot ta learn." He turned around to lead them onwards. "All in good time, mates." He said as they began walking behind him.

Their footfalls echoed throughout the empty cavern as they walked onwards. Jasselbad held the lead, using Dafierno's battleaxe as a walking stick as he went. Casper walked cautiously behind. Even if Jasselbad was in neutral alliance, his dishonest appearance made him suspicious in the visitor's eyes. Isabella clung to Poncho, slightly scared to be in such a hellish place. The stone corridor led them deeper and deeper into the volcano's side. Steam spewed out of cracks, heating bare skin as they passed by. Torches lit the pathway, casting shadows about and entertaining the dark.

"Ah, alright then, here we are." Jasselbad stated as they neared the end of the walkway. Opening to a new room, the path let out to a magnificent cavern. Stopping at the entrance, they looked around at Jasselbad's living quarters. There was no doubt that he lived simply but still comfortably. A fire pit, letting off small puffs of smoke was dug next to a straw mat in the corner, suggesting that it was his sleeping area. A larger fire pit took up a large amount of space in the center of the cavern. Cluttered with bones and graced with a spit, they knew he used it for cooking. A squat chair with a hole in the center hid in the dark, shrouded with old dirty rags, was an obvious area that Jasselbad used that area as a makeshift bathroom. Though primitive in appearance, it looked like a livable situation.

"You live alone here?" Casper asked curiously.

"Nah, I live 'ere weth Sheila. Hey, Sheila, c'mon down girl!" Jasselbad looked up and shouted up toward the ceiling. Tilting his head up, Casper realized that the roof of the cavern was lost in darkness. The only signs of a top were large stalactites jutting down from the top. It would seem that the ceiling reached up higher than it should.

From an unseen creature's lungs, an earsplitting screech emanated from the bizarre darkness above as the sound of rushing air was heard. A giant figure dropped straight down towards them at frightening speeds. As it approached them, giant red wings shot out from its side, breaking its plummet and letting it glide gracefully to the ground. The three visitors watched with terror as a graceful red drake landed its talons on the ground only a few feet from them. Though not as big as the drakes Casper had seen in H'izveral's memories, it was still larger than anything Casper would want to deal with. Lowering its head, the creature craned its neck to look at him viciously.

"Ah this be Sheila. Now Sheila, leave 'em alone. They're our guests, not yer dinner." Sheila gave Jasselbad a disappointed glare before stalking off to a wall where she found a firm place to lean and rest her massive body.

"Well that explains the large living space." Looking back as he spoke, Casper could see Isabella clutching Poncho for dear life, evidently terrified of Sheila's dangerous appearance, if not from dank feeling of the entire cavern.

"Hey, dun worry, lit'l girl," Jasselbad grinned. "She won't eat cha less I be tellin' her too." He grinned wider as she buried her head into Poncho's comforting torso.

"You just make sure your little pet doesn't eat either of them," Casper snapped defiantly as his eyes burned.

"Oh yeah? Whatcha gonna do bout it, boy?" Jasselbad turned to match the cyspherion's gaze. The two men stood face to face in a staring contest. Realizing his disadvantage in a fight against a seasoned fighter and a drake, Casper broke away, letting Jasselbad triumph. "That's what I thought. Jus ya behave yerself in here. Remember, yer tha guests, not me. It would make it much easier if I were to jus let 'er eat cha mates, instead of makin' her go out huntin' fer her meals."

Casper nodded as he muttered a "yes sir."

"Ser? Dun be callin' me ser!" Jasselbad exploded. "Maybe Jasselbad, yer royal highness, or mighty one?" He waited a moment before breaking into uproarious laughter. "I'm just kiddin' loves. Jus call me Jasselbad, or Jassel." He quieted down to a chuckle as they laughed nervously with him. "Well mateys, make yerselves at home." He spread his arms around the cavern. "One room apartment, but its rent free. Oh, you'll be wantin' to watch out fer tha seismic activity 'round here. We're inside a volcano, remember. Lot's of shakin'.'"

Isabella slowly released her grip on Poncho and darted fear stricken eyes around the room. Poncho let go slightly, still ready to defend her at a moment's notice. They walked out to the center of the room, beginning their exploration of the cavern. Casper kept a close eye on them while they admired the modest living quarters of Jasselbad.

"Thank you for your generous offer, but we're not planning on staying long. I just need you to teach me how to fight and then we'll be off your hands." His look jumped back to the overly muscular host, resuming a defensive stance. In response, Jasselbad threw back his head, roaring in merriment. "You really like laughing, don't you?" Casper asked, puzzled at the angel's response.

"Ay, that I do," he answered, wiping tears from his face. "Looks like you've been makin' me laugh a bet too hard. Now, do ya really think ya could show up fer jus' a few hours and learn how ta fight? Nah it's gonna take a lot longer than that. We'll get started on yer training right away though, if yer that anxious ta get out. Now first, we be needin' ta talk 'bout payment. Yer ready to give me whateva I want from ya?"

"Nacafentu said you owed him a debt and you training me would repay it. So I guess I owe you nothing?"

"Aw, Nacafentu, that ole' fool's been hangin' upside down lit'l too long. Mates, I'll tell ya what though. His debt were repaid when I didn' kill ya. It's gonna take a lot more than that ta learn my secrets." Casper began wrapping his knuckles around the machete at his belt, preparing to draw it. The actions caught Jasselbad's attention, making him look nonchalantly down to the sword. "Now dun be thinkin' anythen rash now. Ferst of, that little sliver of metal ain't doin' ya no good. Ya be needin' a big boy's weapon now." He placed his hand on Casper's as he spoke, stopping him from drawing the blade any further. "Second of all, I only be needin' three things from ya. First one ya already gave me, by seekin' me out and comin' in here." He turned away and started walking towards the back of the cave.

"Wait, what are the other two?" Casper yelled after him, slightly aggravated.

"Give it time. You'll be findin' out soon enough." He turned only slightly to give his response. "Now come on, let's find ya a suitable weapon." Casper followed him to the back of the cavern where Jasselbad was pushing firmly against the stone wall. With great resistance, a slab of stone moved out of place and slid inwards on hidden tracks. Fully opened, it showed Casper a new, smaller cavern, filled with all types of bizarre weapons, some he couldn't even recognize. Jasselbad went right in and began shuffling through them intently.

"We'll be needin' somethin' fit fer the mighty cyspherion," He rambled as weapons were shifted by his huge hands. Casper looked at each piece of metal with a new appreciation, only to be disappointed when Jasselbad tossed it deftly away. He had no idea how to wield half of them weapons in the room, but each one looked better and more deadly than the last. After what seemed like forever, Jasselbad paused in his search.

"Ah, tha perfect weapons fer ya."

"Weapons?"

"That right, why limit yerself ta jus' one now? Here ya go." Looking back to where Jasselbad had been searching, Casper saw two matching short swords shinning brilliantly in his hands. They looked perfectly balanced and decorated with beautiful etchings up and down the blade, which looked very much like the dagger that was used to kill Alyssa. "Ah, they be twin short swords, made from blue drake bones. They'll be yer best friends from now on. You are graceful yet strong, perfect combination ta be lethal, once I show ya how." He smiled as Casper slid his fingers on the hilts of the matching weapons.

"Yeah, go on and take 'em. They're yers now." Casper grinned as Jasselbad let his hands fall off of them, letting Casper take full hold on their smooth handles. Holding one in each hand, he let the blades sing through the air as he felt the weight and balance points of both swords.

"They're beautiful," he uttered as each blade swung around empty air.

"Yeah, they suit ya well, no doubt bout that. Now ya can get rid of tha' useless scrap of metal on yer belt." He pulled two leather scabbards from the pile and held them up for inspection. "These'll hold 'em for ya." Remembering that he wasn't the only one in the room, Casper shook the day dream from his mind and looked down toward the old machete at his side. Nodding, he gently placed the new weapons on the ground, taking great care to not scuff or damage either one. Pulling the old machete from his belt, he tossed it carelessly back into the main cavern. Poncho heard the clattering sound of metal and instantly picked it up hastily before returning to Isabella's side to continue their self-guided tour. Meanwhile, Casper fastened the leather scabbards to his belt, admiring their own uniquely dazzling designs. Picking up his new weapons, he strode out of the back room, beaming with pride as a sword stood at ready in each hand.

"Ya ready to start yer training then?" Casper heard from behind him. He nodded slowly, without turning. "Alright, lesson one then, try an' hit me." Just as soon as he heard the words he spun around, swords up in a guard stance only to find Jasselbad a few paces away. Holding the axe in a practiced stance, the old angel stared back at him in a somber smile. "An' dun be holdin' back, Give it all ya got."

Casper's face turned instantly serious. He took two steps forward and swung his left arm toward the angel, leaving his right hand up to guard the chest area. Jasselbad quickly blocked the blow with his axe handle as he spun it around. Continuing the spin overhand, he brought it swiftly around and down at Casper's feet, tripping him.

"Looks like we got a ways to go, eh?" Jasselbad asked as he stood over his fallen opponent with his axe in a threatening position.

Chapter 18

"Again!" The harsh sound of Jasselbad's scratchy voice made Casper flinch. It had been two months since the two had met and there was still no sign of progress in his lessons.

"Can't we just move on? You haven't taught me anything new in the past six weeks."

"No, yer too rigid! Ya need ta loosen up an feel yer powers flow through yer body!"

"You can't do it, don't see how you're such an expert." Casper growled under his breath.

"An' thar's the door, mate. I keep no prisoners. Yer free ta leave anytime ya want. Ya know I can only tap inta neutral powers. You can use all three of 'em. Good, evil, or neutral." Grumbling in irritation, Casper reset his stance to prepare for yet another of the endless cycle of exercises that had been drilled into his head.

He slid his feet apart until they were exactly two and half feet apart and parallel to each other. Shifting his weight to a central balance point, he found the all too comfortable position that haunted his legs every practice session. Then he held his swords near his hips with the blades pointing at forty five degrees away from his body.

"Good, now get ready." Casper glanced angrily towards Jasselbad who lounged in a stone chair. "Eyes ferward, stay focused!" he snapped as Casper twisted his head back to look at the opposite wall. Closing his eyes slightly, he could feel the intense wave of energy beginning to channel through his veins. Rage and hatred found its way to his left arm while on the right arm he allowed love and compassion to flow gracefully until it found his knuckles. Opening both eyes slowly, he felt a total calm overcome his entire body. The sword in his left hand began to glow a bright red as the one in his right glowed blue. The encompassing feelings washed through his veins, giving him extra strength.

"alright, now let 'er go." Casper took a sweeping step forward with his right leg and extended his arms straight outwards, keeping the blades pointing up. Pivoting in a fluid motion, he loosened all of the muscles in his body, lowering the already low stance. Swinging his right hand above his head, Casper let the blade go behind his back. He continued circling his arm backwards, bringing the sword around with it. As it approached the ground, he let it touch the sandy surface lightly, leaving a blue trail of fire in its wake. Letting it go past its original position, Casper let the blade stray up into the air and brought the sword in his left hand around in a circle. He mirrored the first blade's movements with his left hand, leaving red fire in a similar path. Bringing attention back to his right hand, Casper swung it directly over his head. He then brought his body closer to the ground by buckling his right knee. While doing so, he swung the right handed blade directly in front of him, letting the tip of it brush the ground and giving him another blue line parallel to his body. This elaborate motion brought the blade high into the air. Lifting his right leg off of the ground, Casper arced the blade once again over his head and down along the ground, starting from the first trail of blue fire but changing course drastically to connect where the last trail had ended.

He dropped his leg back to the earth as the blade departed the ground. Lifting his left foot up high, he once again mirrored the path with his left hand, starting from the back and bringing it forward to join the blue trail in front. As he dropped the raised foot gracefully onto the ground, he pointed both swords towards the earth. He then spun around, letting the blades strike the ground in a giant circle of blue and red fire. After rotating all the way around, he brought the glowing swords back to his chest, blades pointing toward the ceiling. Extending his arms straight out, he paused when they stood perfectly aligned with the floor. Flicking his wrists, he watched in anticipation and quickly turning into disappointment as nothing happened.

"Look at yer feet." Casper fought the sigh of anger while he checked to see what he already knew. "That pentagram should be full, or else it don't work." As mad as he was, Casper knew Jasselbad was right. After practicing the same moves over and over again, he still could not master making a perfect pentagram. He tried harder and harder every day, but the lines of fire never matched up perfectly. Groaning, he reset his position to prepare for another practice.

After failing miserably for the seventh time that day, Jasselbad finally allowed Casper to stop for a break. Glad to be able to stop, he trudged over to the crudely formed rock chairs near the main fire pit where Poncho was hard at work teaching Isabella English.

"How's the progress over here?" he asked, slumping into the nearest free seat and leaning the swords by his side.

"Better than yours," Isabella answered, beaming with pride. "I can speak pretty good now." She concentrated on each word, making sure it was the right one to use before actually saying it. Casper sighed, trying to hide his irritation as Poncho laughed. He sat in silence and listened as Poncho began to once again instruct Isabella on English words.

After playing with his tattered clothes for a moment, he suddenly looked down to where his shirt hung. It had long since ripped and stained beyond recognition. The sleeves had been torn off and the tear down the center of his chest was now unraveling, letting loose threads hang all about. The entire shirt was drenched in sweat, causing it to cling to his muscular chest as he breathed in and out. Leading his eyes further down, he could see his pants worn away by having worn them constantly. Holes ran through the pair of jeans letting his skin show through in multiple areas. What wasn't ripped was heavily caked in dirt and grime. Poncho and Isabella were in no better condition. Two months in a volcano had done its work on them and their clothing. They kept clean only by a heated spring that bubbled up in an adjoining cavern.

Not learning the techniques had bothered Casper. It was his fault they were stuck there so long. If he could only master the arts, they could finally leave this dismal place.

"It's been two months and we have no idea how much longer this is going to take," Casper grunted as he interrupted Isabella's lessons. "Why don't you take Isabella back to the town? You can get cleaned up and into some proper clothes." Poncho and Isabella stared at him with uncertainty as he spoke with words filled in guilt.

"No, we in this together," Poncho snapped, jumping to his feet. "I not going to leave you alone. You the only friend I got now, beside Isabella." He turned and stared deeply into his lover's eyes.

"But what about her parents, they're going to be worried about her by now." The two Mexicans shot glances down at the ground in silence. Watching a tear drop from Isabella's face, he felt suddenly ashamed for what he had done. "Oh no, I'm so sorry," He said apologetically, reaching out and comforting her with a hug. "I didn't realize. You can stay here with us."

"It alright," she answered, smiling a little. "I barely knew them myself. They disappeared one night when I was a little girl. I was left to..." She turned to Poncho, searching for the right words.

"Fend for yourself?"

"Fend for myself, with help of the village." She spoke with a slight sniffle, still tearing slightly at the thought of her parent's disappearance. "No one probably know I missing."

"Well you guys can at least go outside and find yourselves a decent meal. Something other than whatever that slop Jasselbad's been feeding us may do wonders for your stomach." As Casper spoke, he pointed over toward the pot of porridge like liquid set near the fire. "Jasselbad may be alright for a fallen angel, but he's certainly no cook." Poncho and Isabella readily agreed with his comment and headed for the door. As Casper leaned back to relax, an ear-splitting groan escaped from the creature behind him. "You too, Sheila," Casper responded without turning around. "Keep an eye on them and make sure they don't get into trouble. You should also find something better to eat for yourself too." Shrieking in delight, she launched herself into the air, heading for the roof high above. Even though Casper couldn't see up that high, he knew that there was an exit and entry point somewhere high above. Too big to fit through the cavern's walkways, she had to use the holes in the ceiling in order to escape to open air.

Smiling with relief, Casper leaned back in his chair, enjoying the break he had from being drilled constantly. How much longer he wondered, would he be in here? The exercise he was on wasn't incredibly hard and someone like himself should have been able to do it from the beginning. He opened his eyes and surveyed the room. Jasselbad had taken off, probably in search of more food to torment them with.

Rising to his feet, he took a sword in each hand and walked to an open spot on the floor. He then turned to face the pot containing porridge. Breathing in deeply, his mind cleared to a surreal calmness. The emptiness within him instantly filled with images of Aspriel and Justine. He concentrated on them and felt energy flow to his hands. Opening his eyes, he saw the world as a blur while his muscles moved independently from his mind. He felt as if he was letting both of his mothers down by staying here. He felt rage while he grew angrier and angrier at his own inhibitions. He still needed to avenge Aspriel's death and without him being in Heresen, who was going to protect Justine? Jesse could protect her but for only so long and definitely not if anyone found out her association with him. A shattering sound brought him back to reality. His vision cleared to an exciting sight as porridge covered metal shards flew about in the cave. The porridge sludged slowly into the fire pit where it sizzled and crackled in the dancing flames.

A clapping sound made Casper turn to the cavern's entrance. Jasselbad stood stoutly in the doorway, applauding his student's actions as he laughed aloud.

"I git it, ya don't like my cookin' now do ya? Shoulda thought ta use that as a target in tha practice sessions. Well dun jus be standin' there gapin', look down at yer feet." Tilting his head down, Casper could see that his feet were surrounded by a perfectly drawn glowing pentagram. Shock turned to joy as he realized that they could finally move on. He walked briskly away from the flames, which promptly extinguished upon him leaving the symbol.

"I'm ready, show me what's next." He walked to his mentor, smiling with pride.

"Damn straight yer ready," the old angel replied while his demeanor turned serious. "Ya destroyed my best pot. I got a good mind ta make ya get me a new one." He scowled at the metallic remains smoldering in porridge. "But ya dun't got time ta git me one. We got work ta do." He laughed while slapping Casper's back. "Back ta the exercise field. Time fer ya to learn a new move, mate." They walked joyfully back into the cavern, Jasselbad beaming with pride for his apprentice while Casper grinned, eager to learn his new move.

~~~~~~~~~~~~~~~~~~~~~~~~~~~~~~~~~

Poncho burst through the door and into the sulfurous air around the volcano's mouth. He gripped Isabella's hand tightly as she was led upwards to the top. Walking carefully, they traversed the staircase and made it safely over the side. Standing just a few inches from the mouth, they stopped to stare into each other's eyes. The couple shared a moment together as love floated between their faces. Leaning in, Poncho closed his eyes and pursed his lips for a kiss. Isabella started leaning in only to start giggling instead. She pecked his lips with hers before running at full speed down the side of the volcano.

"Hey!" Poncho yelled, chasing down after her. "I'm going to catch you!" He laughed, trying to keep her in his sight. Laughing, Isabella rushed through the dead vegetation, easily staying ahead of Poncho who was hindered by the dead branches and burnt brush in his way. She reached the line where plants were able to grow and quickly disappeared inside. Running excitedly about, she found a perfect hiding spot to duck into. Holding her hand over her mouth, she held back her laughing as Poncho jumped into view, yelling for her to come out.

Pausing just near her, she could see his legs only inches from her nose. He was no longer the skinny awkward boy she had met years ago. Instead his body now bulged slightly with muscles, making him even more attractive then when he had to leave for America. She plucked a tall fern from nearby and began brushing it lightly on the boy's leg as he looked around with a puzzled look. Feeling the fern on his calf, he spun and pounced toward her hiding spot.

"Gotcha!" He yelled as his long arms pinned her against the ground. Wrestling his strong body away, she forced him to roll over and jumped on top of his chest. They pushed against each other, trying to win the bout while laughing the entire time. They rolled through the jungle, crashing over small plants and roots until sweaty and tired, they laid down next to each other. Their lips touched passionately as romance swept through the area. Their embrace however, was short lived.

A shadow washed over them, making them feel uneasy. Sitting up, they both searched for the source. The thing blocking the sun glared down at them. Darkened by the shadows, neither one of the terrified children could see its features clearly. They did know though that there were dangers associated with this visitor. Cowering in terror, Isabella backed away from the creature as Poncho drew his dagger and machete. Although not well trained with them, he had been practicing with them by himself in the volcano while alone.

Wielding them in the most menacing way possible, he stood his ground against whatever was in front of him. The face came closer as it bent over for a better look. Poncho took a small step backwards in defense as the Minotaur snorted in his face, letting its stench fall on their faces.

A thick golden ring punctured the creature's nostrils and Poncho could see the mucus coating it bore from years of ill treatment. The monster's fur was ragged and matted as it probably had never been washed. Horns, stained with blood, sprouted through the greasy hair on its head. Bullish eyes glared with the hunger of human flesh as they sized up the boy in front of him. His gigantic left arm stood at ready by his side while his right hand clutched a flail. Holding desperately onto what little courage he had, Poncho steadied his weapons and held them near the minotaur's face. The giant seemed to chuckle at Poncho's weak attempts of protection.

Panic shot through Poncho, rooting him to the spot as the minotaur stood back upright and roared in delight as he prepared for the kill.

Chapter 19

Hair whipped through the air as the minotaur's head descended back towards Poncho with intentions of tearing the head clean off his shoulders. Bigger than what Poncho would have suspected the minotaur species to be, it stood a tall as a tree and looked as if it could rip one out the ground. Its massive head flew towards the children as he bent over. Gaping jaws closed down around Poncho, encasing him in its horrendous mouth. In desperation, he slashed madly at the monster's tongue, letting blood spew from the giant muscle. As the minotaur lashed its sliced tongue about, he withdrew his gigantic head from the ground, shrieking in pain and anger. Too distracted by his wounds, he didn't see Poncho take the opportunity to force his dagger into an unprotected kneecap, making him howl as the hilt stopped on his furry skin.

Taking a step back, he jerked the metal free from Poncho's hands and stumbled around, smashing into trees as he went. Poncho seized another opportunity to strike the hairy monster. As the enraged creature smashed around clumsily, Poncho clutched the machete and reinforced it with both hands as he jumped past the uninjured leg, sliding the sword blade against its skin upon passing. Blood shot forcefully against his face as he landed nimbly behind the minotaur.

Jumping out of the way, Poncho watched him fall backwards, knocking down a nearby tree as he slammed into the ground. Poncho instantly jumped on top of the fallen opponent and smiled wickedly.

"Who's the tough guy now?" Slicing viciously with the machete, Poncho ripped at the creature's chest cavity. Yowling in pain, the minotaur squirmed with each hit, trying to fling the small boy off of his stomach. Anger set in and he raised his flail off the ground. Trying to catch the little boy off guard, he swung it swiftly toward Poncho who was still preoccupied on his chest. Poncho, seeing the flail from the corner of his eye, ducked just as it passed over his head, missing his skull by only a few inches. Not waiting for a second pass, Poncho leapt from the chest to his head, planting the machete into the cornea of his left eye. Twisting the metal about in the eye socket, he gripped the sword tightly to keep his balance while the beast swung his head in agony. With a tremendous turn, the minotaur finally flung Poncho from his face, pulling the machete with him.

Air escaped Poncho's lungs as he was forced against a nearby tree. Having the breath knocked out of him, he could do no more than slide down the tree's trunk and clutch his stomach in pain. While Poncho tried to regain his bearings, the monster rose unsteadily to his feet, shaking the pain from his body and letting adrenaline pump through his system. Giving a mighty roar, he prepared for an attack just moments before his head disappeared from his shoulders.

As the beheaded corpse crumbled to the ground in front of Poncho, it revealed a delighted Sheila who munched happily on the minotaur's skull bone.

"Good girl," Poncho heaved through labored breathing. Letting a grin spread across his countenance, he lifted himself into a standing position and walked over to Sheila who was still chewing her food as he approached. He gingerly rubbed his hand across the softer red scales of her stomach in appreciation. While marveling at the giant scales shining in the bright daylight, he laughed at the soft, almost purring sound she made in response to being rubbed.

After making sure the jungle was safe around them, Isabella stepped carefully next to Poncho and joined him in stroking Sheila's underbelly. The enormous drake continued to purr in delight as she delved into the minotaur's body, searching for the best and most delectable meat to free from the carcass.

~~~~~~~~~~~~~~~ • ~~~~~~~~~~~~~~~

The three friends sat together on the jungle floor. Poncho and Isabella shared romantic secrets while Sheila feasted on the Minotaur's body parts. The sun had begun to set, casting shadows around them as Poncho and Isabella lay together against Sheila's stomach. The insects about them chirped in unison, forming a song of sorts and giving them a magically enchanting tune for them to lose their thoughts in.

"We should be gettin' back," Poncho sighed, breaking the rhythmic sounds. "They'll be worryin' bout us." Isabella nodded as she leaned in for one more kiss before standing up. "Too bad we never found food for ourselves." He continued, breaking his lips from her kiss. "Look like we'll be eatin' Jasselbad's slop again tonight." Isabella grimaced as she remembered the tasteless porridge waiting for them back in the volcano.

"Maybe we can still find somethin' to eat?" She asked hopefully as she looked around. Dusk was falling and it was getting hard to see anything clearly. "Before it gets any darker?"

"Alright, we'll see what we can find, but quick." Even though night was closing in, Poncho was not totally sure he could stomach another night of Jasselbad's cooking and was willing to take his chances with the wildlife. Besides, with Sheila with them they would be safe from any more harm.

Poncho led Isabella through the undergrowth while they foraged for a sensible dinner. Sheila, being larger then the rest, stomped happily behind, keeping a close eye on her friends and hoping another meal would come along before they returned to her master in the volcano.

A bird flew lazily about overhead, screeching loudly as they traversed the jungle floor. The fading twilight made it increasingly harder for them to see and Poncho did not see the berry bush until he had finally tripped over it.

"Watch out," he called back. "There's a bush over here." Twisting his body around, he felt for the scraggly branches reaching out from the ground and snagging on Poncho's pants leg. "Gomuvas" He yelled out as his hands closed around the familiar fruit. "Our mouths are saved, at least for tonight."

Isabella sat down next to him and began greedily grabbing at the new found fruit. Watching them curiously, Sheila lay her body down in a guarding position, wondering why they ate the nauseating fruit from the ground. The Minotaur proved to be a much better meal and she would have surely shared the meat if they wanted it. Juice dripped down the children's chins as they greedily chewed their precious food, laughing uncontrollably at each other. Knowing Sheila was with them made it feel like a safe haven. She was big enough to protect them from anything that would pass by and most predators would avoid a drake her size.

Finally satisfied, Poncho and Isabella left the Gomuva bush, pocketing a few for later. They walked blindly to where Sheila sat patiently.

"Come on girl, you're going to have to lead us back." It was a new moon and even a trained human eye would have trouble picking out the path in the complete darkness. Sheila, on the other hand could see in the blackest night and would be able to sense their way back even without light.

Nudging the two onto her back, Sheila let them climb up onto her neck. Once she was sure they were seated properly she turned her head up towards the heavens and released a large fireball from her lungs, burning a perfect path through the branches to launch from. Rearing onto her hind legs she beat her wings against the ground, getting enough momentum for take-off. Isabella, lurching from the sudden movement, tightened her arms around Poncho's torso as Sheila took to the air.

Poncho forgot his acrophobia and threw his head back to laugh as the wind swept his hair back into an uncertain Isabella's face. Looking down caused her to clench her arms tighter around Poncho's stomach while she shivered in fear. Isabella, like Poncho, had always been afraid of heights and riding above the jungle on a drake's back was no exception. Feeling her tightened grip on his torso, Poncho let go of Sheila's scales with one hand and reached back to comfort her. When she realized there was no current danger, she loosened her grip and began to enjoy the ride, at least until they reached the volcano's side. Being invisible to the naked eye, neither Poncho nor Isabella could make out the tiny crevice that served as Sheila's doorway. Screaming in terror, the two watched as Sheila rapidly approached the molten rock below. Just as they were about to dive straight into the bubbling liquid, she broke the fall and soared through the gap, barely scraping the rocky sides with her wingtips as she passed through.

Realizing what was going on, the two passengers quickly ducked so they wouldn't get knocked off of their ride and into the magma chamber below. They kept their heads down until the cool air of Jasselbad's cavern surrounded them. Bracing against Sheila, they watched the stony floor below approach as she rapidly plummeted in a freefall. Unfolding her wings once again, she pulled up and landed gracefully onto the ground and bent down low to let her riders off.

"Ah, so yer back, finally? Bout time." Everyone turned to see Jasselbad leaning carelessly against the wall while holding a piece of straw in between his teeth. "Thought ya'd be runnin' off on us." He chuckled as Sheila took a few steps over to Jasselbad. Craning her head down, she let the fallen angel pet her snout, cooing happily. "Ah that's a good gerl. Ya make shure they didn' get in trouble then?" She nodded slowly, still enjoying his hand on her scales.

"So how's Casper doin'?" Poncho winced, scared to hear the same report they had been getting the past couple of months.

"Well," Jasselbad started as he walked past Sheila's head. "Why don't ya take a look yerself?" Sheila, turning her head, watched as her master walked past her towards the two strange fruit eating kids. "He's right ov'r thar, loves." The place Jasselbad pointed to was inhabited by Casper, deep in focus and oblivious to the world. Surrounding the preoccupied cyspherion were lines of fire. They watched in wonder as he began another set of slashes, creating more intricate patterns about the room. A beautiful sight befell them as the light burned around them in astounding creations. Red and blue mixed in startling ways before dying out to make room for new flame lines.

"He finally got it?" Poncho asked as he marveled at the fires. "He learned what you were teaching him?"

"Yep mates, he finally loosen'd up and learnt ta control his feelins'."

"So what he doing now?"

"Ah, he be playin' now. Tossin' tha flames about and gettin' a feel fer them. Tha more he gits used to 'em, tha better off he'll be."

Silence ensued, letting Casper practice in silence as the air about them radiated in a strange glow until after what seemed like hours, he stopped for a break.

"Well, what do you think?" He asked as sweat dripped from his forehead. He had overdone the workout and was saturated with his own salty sweat from head to toe. "Have I done well enough to please you?" A smile crossed his lips as the words fought though deep panting. Sighing heavily, he slid the blades into the scabbards on his hips.

"Ya've done well my friend," Jasselbad answered as he returned the smile with a slightly darker tone. "Ya even gave me yer second sacrifice." Casper looked at him with a questioning stare. "Tha second one was yer time. Ya spent it with me." Casper smiled once again, patting Jasselbad on his shoulder.

"Alright then, looks like I'm done here." He stated, walking around him in an attempt to leave.

"Now hold on thar. I rememba askin' fer three things from ya. Now as I see it, I've only gotten two. That means thar's still one thing ya need ta give me."

Casper turned around to look at Jasselbad who had been eying the kids curiously. "Don't you dare hurt either one of them." Casper warned, stepping in between Jasselbad and Poncho, who decidedly assumed a protective stance in front of Isabella, holding his machete at ready. "I'll give you a matching scar if you come near them." Casper drew his swords from their homes in his belt, getting ready to fend off any attack from Jasselbad.

"Now don't ya worry, I have no interest in hurtin' them. Thar my friends now and I wouldn' dream of hurtin' 'em. Now let me see yer two swords thar." He held his hands out, beckoning for the swords that were being held with the points towards his body. Looking slightly apprehensive, Casper slowly turned the hilts toward the angel forfeited his weapons to Jasselbad.

"But I thought you said these were mine?" Casper asked as the handles left his unwilling fingers. "I can't keep them?" Jasselbad chuckled a little at Casper's reaction to his request.

"Now love, I neva said ya couldn't keep 'em. I just wanted ta see 'em fer a moment." He examined the swords closely, keeping a smile on his face as he did so. Looking up, his grin widened. Before Casper saw any movement, he could feel the cold steel work its way through his chest cavity. Looking down, he saw that the two swords he was so used to were now being plunged further and further into his chest, letting his thick blood flow down the metal. Snorting at the pain, Casper could do no more than cough up blood as the weapons slid all the way through his body.

"What are you doin'?" He heard Poncho yell behind him just shortly after the blades penetrated his back and burst into open air.

"Now ya two just stay thar like good little kids. Ya don't want ta mess with me, or you'll be sorry." These were the fading words Casper heard come from Jasselbad as he slumped down. Suspended by the metal blades, he turned limp and was held up only by Jasselbad's raw strength. Spitting out blood, his world went dark as he passed out from the pain.

Chapter 20

Casper groaned loudly as he felt his head starting to clear. Not knowing how long he had been unconscious made him feel even groggier and he could hear loud whispers falling down around him, making him experience a headache with each word. Throbbing from the pain, his face grimaced as he tried to open heavy eyelids. As his vision finally cleared, the cavern reappeared before him. Trying to stand up, he suddenly realized that chains, attached to iron shackles on his wrists and ankles, tethered him helplessly to the rock wall. Grunting with effort, he pushed himself all of the way up into a standing position. Casper strained against the cold chains, trying vainly to free himself from bondage but not having all of his strength returned to him, he finally slumped back down in defeat.

"He's awake!" Looking up toward the voice, he could see a rickety metal cage just above holding Poncho and Isabella captive. The two children looked down at Casper as he tried once again to pull the chains free of the wall. "We thought he had killed you." Poncho shouted. "I try to stop him but he took my sword away and locked us in this cage."

Casper gave up his tug of war with the chains after another round of futile attempts gave him no freedom. "What does he want? Why'd he do this to us?"

"I don't know, he just left us like this, mumbled somethin' about waitin' for you to wake up and took off. Only left his pet to watch us." Jutting his finger out defiantly, Poncho pointed to the sleeping drake. Curled up in a ball, she seemingly was content with her job as a guard dog. She looked up lazily at the mention of her name before lowering her head back with a puff of smoke. "Yeah that right, don't even look at us. I thought you were our friend!" Poncho punctuated his yelling by shaking his fist in the air as he spoke to the giant beast.

"Well what's with all tha commotion in here?" The sound of Jasselbad's voice announced his approach as he entered from a nearby passage. "I was hopin' ya'd all get along, yer al friends here." Sneering, he walked in and patted Sheila on the head, who cooed in response to the angel. "Now don' be yellin' at poor ole' Sheila here. She be likin' ya all, like family."

"Shut up and let us go!" Poncho yelled from his cage.

"Now I can't be doin' that just yet. Ya see I still have somethin' to do."

"You mean like sell me to the highest bidder, you two faced liar!" Casper pulled against the chains as he tried once again freeing himself so he could attack Jasselbad.

"Now Why would ya think somethin' like that?" He grinned while walking towards Casper. Stopping just before the chained man, the fallen angel's face glowed with an evil shine. "Ya don' trust me then, do ya?" He slid two swords from behind his back as he finished off his question. Casper gasped in anger as the all too familiar blades sung in unison. Stepping back half a step, Jasselbad swung the blades in two arcs, testing them right in front of him. For two months Casper had been training with those weapons and undoubtedly had become attached to them. He now longed for them to return in his own hands. Red liquid dripped thickly off the metallic arcs as they spun in the air and as Casper watched them slicing through the air, he quickly realized it was his blood still fresh on the blades.

Walking forward, Jasselbad brought the swords closer and closer to Casper, who closed his eyes and awaited the oncoming doom of metal. Unable to move from his spot on the wall, Casper had no chance of protecting himself and still weakened by the fresh cuts in his stomach only furthered to worsen the situation. As the blades came near his face, Casper could hear their wielder chuckling. Only inches from Casper, he held his breath and awaited death but the blades never made contact with his skin. Instead, the sound of metal breaking metal filled the room as Casper felt the chains give way, spilling his body onto the floor.

Snapping his eyes open, he looked up to see Jasselbad just above him, still grinning. The floor felt damp and cold on Casper's hands. With a grunt he quickly pushed himself into a standing position. Looking with apprehension at his mentor, he watched Jasselbad hold his hands out, offering the sword handles to Casper.

"What the hell are you doing?" Shrinking away from the swords, Casper made it obvious that he didn't trust the ambiguous angel.

"I'm given ya yer weapons back. Doncha want 'em?" He stood unmoving, waiting for Casper to respond. With uncertain hands, he wrapped his fingers around the hilts, pulling them slowly free of Jasselbad's grip. "Now that's a good boy. Ya learned well from me."

"Why'd you try to kill me?"

"I weren't tryin' ta kill no one. Ya suffer from tha curse of Prometheus."

"Prometheus, you mean the titan from myths that brought mankind fire?"

"Ya, in a sense anyway. Prometheus were a mercenary much like myself an' tha fire were intelligence. He convinced man and woman ta eat tha fruits of knowledge."

"I thought it was Satan who told Adam and Eve to eat the apple of knowledge?"

"Nah, that be what Zeus wanted yer to believe. Prometheus wanted humans ta be able ta think fer themselves. This was ferbidden by GOD himself though. When he caught wind of it, he came down ta examine what had happened. He angrily demanded that whoever were responsible would step forward. Now Prometheus were brave, but were not about go up against GOD. He stayed hidden and watched as GOD unfurled his wrath. He cursed both sides and any neutral creatures fer the defiance against him. Although all tha creatures are hard ta kill, almost immortal, they had ta pay. In order fer us to kill anythin' with cold steel, tha metal must first drink from our blood."

"So we have to coat our weapons in our own blood to kill anything?"

"Right love, now ya can feel yer life force in these very blades, they belong ta you."

"So what happens if we don't bleed on the weapon?"

"Tha creature ya tried ta kill would be healed by GOD's graces. He would give yer opponent its life back."

"So that's why the cougar didn't die." Casper thought as he suddenly remembered the amazing encounter in the jungle. "I never left any blood on the machete. That also explains why that bastard Wyburn cut his wrists just before he killed my mother."

Jasselbad stepped forward and rested a hand on Casper's shoulder. "Listen. I was thar that day. I had been helpin' out Zeus that battle. Wyburn's not ta blame fer yer mother's death. He did what had ta be done. Yer mother was foolish ta kill Dafierno like that. It be against Zeus' code ta be killin' enemies who surrender ta him." Casper looked angrily back at Jasselbad as he tried comforting the cyspherion's memories.

"Zeus' codes be damned!" He spat, pushing the hand roughly off of his shoulder. "It was no reason to kill my mother. Now her murderer must pay. I'll avenge her death. I'll even kill Zeus himself if he gets in my way!"

"Killin' them ain't gonna bring yer parents back. Thar dead and ain't nothin' ya can do bout it. Let tha past be tha past."

"To hell with your morals." Casper felt the red, sticky fluid dripping from the cross guards onto his wrists, distracting his thoughts of vengeance. "Why didn't you just tell me I needed to soak the swords in my blood?" He glared at his mentor with a new rage.

"Well its more fun thes way. Seein' tha surprise on yer face is priceless.

"So you almost killed me without warning to please yourself? What the hell is your problem you sick twisted..." Casper clenched his teeth as he spoke. In the frustration of finding the right words, he instead thrust the twin blades in a crossing pattern just in front of Jasselbad's throat, causing the angel to take a step backwards.

"Now hold on a second thar, Casper. It weren't all fer my enjoyement. Ya see, tha more traumatizin' the wound is, the stronger yer weapons will be."

Casper eased the swords from Jasselbad's neck. "So you did it to make my weapons more powerful?"

"That be right. I did it ta help ya out. You'll be more powerful now. Ya destiny is ta end this war, and you'll be needin' all tha help ya can get."

"What about them?" Without turning, Casper pointed his left sword up towards the metal cage which still trapped Poncho and Isabella. They had been quiet up to this point, but now being indirectly addressed, they yelled protests while rocking the cage back and forth.

"Eh ya, about them..." Jasselbad walked over to the fire pit where Dafierno's battle axe stood waiting. Heaving it onto one shoulder, he continued on toward a section of the wall where an obvious crack ran down the side. With a grunt he plunged the gigantic ax blade deeply into the crevice. Twisting in effort, Jasselbad pushed the battle axe along the crack, letting it scrape along the stone sides. Casper heard metal gears grinding and looking up, saw the cage coming down. Sidestepping out of the way, he moved away from it as it came crashing to a less than perfect landing.

"You guys alright?" The cyspherion rushed over to the fallen cage. With a mighty swing of his swords, he slashed the door open and freed the trapped children.

"Yeah we're good," Poncho huffed as he pulled himself from the wreck. Turning around, he held out his hand and helped Isabella from the cage. Standing tall, the two kids brushed themselves off, coughing slightly from the dust as it sparkled in the dim fire light. Finally satisfied with their appearance, the three of them returned to Jasselbad, who had been leaning on the protruding axe handle, smiling with satisfaction.

"There something wrong with you, man." Poncho spat at him. "Why you got to cage us up there just to get your laughs?"

"Hey, I did that fer yer protection. You'd be tryin' ta kill me an' all I wus doin' wus helpin' out poor ole' Casper here. Ya can have yer machete back now by tha way." He extended one of his gnarled fingers over to where he had carelessly discarded the sword earlier. "Though I'd barely even consider it a weapon, more like a toothpick if ya ask me." Poncho looked from Jasselbad to the sword he was pointing to, hesitating to decide if moving was such a good idea. With a hopeful glance, he stole a look at the cavern that contained Jasselbad's cache of mighty weaponry.

"Now I'd give ya one of mine, but they fer stronger beings then yerself. Sorry son, but yer just not strong enough ta wield somethin' like that." Jasselbad rested a hand on Poncho's head, rustling his hair as he spoke. Poncho only sighed in disappointment, beginning his walk toward his machete and letting Jasselbad's hand swing loosely back to his side.

Spinning slowly back around, Jasselbad gripped the axe handle with both hands and pulled with a strenuous grunt, freeing the weapon from the hole in the wall. "So ya neva told me then, what name do ya go by?" As he spoke, the sound of the old, broken metal cage could be heard as it was sent back up toward the cavern roof at alarming speeds. Casper watched it until it disappeared into the inky blackness above before giving a response.

"My name's Casper, you know that old man."

"Nah I know what humans call ya, but what about us painrytes?"

"Painrytes, what the hell does that mean?" Casper face twisted into a questioning stare as he mouthed the words over and over.

"Ah ya neva been told what a painryte is then? We be painrytes. Blessed or cursed by GOD himself, we be stronger than human, havin' a superior bloodline."

"So a painryte is someone with a superior bloodline?"

"Ah now ya be gettin' it. And I was beginnin' ta believe ya were slow in tha head." Jasselbad grinned, letting his cruel lips twist into an evil smirk. "But ya still haven't answered my question. What be yer name, Michael or Maverick?"

"What difference does it make? I'd rather just stick with Casper." Turning, he showed nonchalantly that he didn't care what anyone called him. "I've been called Casper for twenty one years now and I've gotten pretty partial to it."

"Ah but yer name dictates what alignment ya hail ta. Claimin' ta be Casper just means yer denouncin' yer bloodlines just ta pretend yer mortal. If ya choose Michael then ya choosin' ta work fer the good of mankind and follow Zeus. Now if ya decide ta be Maverick then ya goin' fer the evil in tha world and want ta help out Cronus."

"Why should something as simple as a name dictate where you are in life? Shouldn't we be able to have one name and believe something totally different?"

"Ya should be proud of yer name!" Jasselbad's nostrils flared as his angered voice echoed throughout the cave. "Yer lucky ta have two. Everyone else be like myself, only havin' one and we don't even have tha decency ta chose our paths. I'm stuck with the name Jasselbad, a neutral party in tha war of good and evil. You get ta chose which side ya likin' ta be on. Embrace that choice, but choose wisely. Thar be darkness down either path and steppin' too far in tha wrong direction could spell doom fer ya."

"Damn this war and to hell with me choosing any paths. All I know is both my parents were killed before I even got to meet them, all because of your stupid squabble of good and evil." Casper spit as he responded, just missing Jasselbad's boot with his saliva.

"Ya won't be feelin' that fer long. This ain't just a war, its yer life. One way or another yer gonna have ta choose." Giving up in defeat, Jasselbad walked away and made his way back to the fire pit's edge. He knew his student was headstrong and getting an answer out of him would be impossible at this point. "By tha time we meet again, I feel you'll be havin' tha answer my friend."

"Who says we'll be meeting again? I don't intend on returning to Mexico."

"Our paths will meet again, love." Jasselbad shook his head slowly, keeping his eyes on the fire as he spoke. "Tha sweet frangrance of war is on tha horizon. Can't ya smell it?

Casper shook his head. Quickly realizing that Jasselbad couldn't see his response, he made his answer audible. "No, and I plan on staying far away from any of your wars. You and Zeus and Cronus can fight your own little battles. Just keep me out of it."

"Won't happen mate. Ya see, yer the cyspherion an' like it or not, yer gonna be a big part of tha war. Ya need ta decide who tha winning side will be. The Wrokthien portals have been opening, their bars have been deteriorating eva since ya left fer Mexico an took yer magic with ya. With angels and demons free once again ta move between worlds, they'll be stoppin' at nothin' ta win." Jasselbad's face grew even more stern while he turned back to Casper. "Yer just a tool of war, they'll use ya ta win an give ya whatever lie it takes ta make their side justified. This is why ya got ta make sure ya choose wisely tha path ahead of you." As he spoke, Jasselbad gave Casper the most serious look he had ever seen on the fallen angel's face.

"I will." He responded quietly after a moment of silence. Although Casper wanted nothing to do with the war, the eyes of Jasselbad made shivers run up and down his spine. He no longer wanted to argue with him after that moment. Walking over to the fire pit, he wrapped a mighty arm around his mentor. "I'm sorry, my friend, I didn't mean to upset you. It just that all of this is happening way too fast and my whole world is turning into one big lie."

Jasselbad gave a mighty roar of laughter, shaking Casper's arm as it radiated through his body. "Now don't worry bout me, mate. It's you I'm worried fer. Ya got tha power ta end this and I want ta make sure ya use it right."

The sound of coughing drew their attention away from each other. An embarrassed Isabella hid her face in Poncho's strong chest as she coughed again. The two laughed together as they walked over to the children, sitting down to join in their company.

"Well looks like ya best be off." Sitting around in a semi circle, they allowed a day to pass, too caught up in their stories to notice the time go by. With heart felt goodbyes, the three friends left Jasselbad and Sheila to continue on with their lives in the volcano as they started their trek back to the village.

"Don' forget!" Jasselbad yelled up the cavern as they walked away. "Choose yer path wisely. They'll be no changin' once ya start down tha path."

"Don't worry, I wont let you down!" A somber silence fell upon the group as they parted Jasselbad's company, lasting all the way to Harbieno. Casper's twin blades cut through the jungle much easier than the machete had. Feeling the power flowing through it, he knew effort was not needed to cut the thick vegetation. Jasselbad had told him the truth, his blood stained blades did far more than he could ever expect of them. Now he only wished Wyburn was within reach so he could use them to exact his revenge. He knew it would come all in due time though and he was already on his way back to Heresen.

Approaching Harbieno's edge, they could see sentries posted all about. The night watches were easily recognized as they held lanterns bright with flickering flames, keeping an eye out on the whole town. Ducking in the thin underbrush, the three of them hid just out of the lantern's glow.

"We will be fine." Isabella chirped in her usual cheerful tone. "They are friends and they will protect us from harm."

"Quiet!" Casper hissed under his breath while grabbing the girl's arm before she could dart out of the bushes. "I don't think they'll be helping us." Bobbin his head sideways, he motioned to the nearest guard. Squinting through the darkness, Isabella could see what he was pointing to. A therion sat at ready near his feet, snarling silently as it curled its lips, but still staying obediently by the guard's side.

"They must be still looking for us. After the airport and then you killing our kidnappers, we must be pretty popular."

"But how would they recognize us? You killed all of them two months ago." They all turned to Isabella, who shrugged with her logic.

"Not all of them." Casper responded after a moment. "Remember what Jasselbad said? I suppose any of the ones I killed with my flames would be dead. But the ones I used the machete on wouldn't have died." He thought for a second. "There were at least two therions I remember that weren't killed by fire." Remembering the creature only a few yards in front of them, Casper realized that it may be a therion that was there that night and would undoubtedly recognize his scent. He pushed Poncho and Isabella back further into the brush as the therion began growling in their direction.

"We'll go another way. We're not safe here." Casper grabbed their arms and pulled them around the edge of the village, darting away from lights and living creatures.

"Where are we going?" Poncho asked as they stumbled through the darkness.

"I need to get back to the airport, but I'm taking the road this time." He stopped suddenly and looked back to Poncho with a hopeful stare. "I can't force you to come back with me, but I really could use a friend's help back in America. We can help change the country and make them realize the error of their ways."

Poncho smiled at his offer. "You know, I got all I need from Mexico right here." Motioning down, he showed off Isabella's hand as her fingers intertwined with his. "All that remains here for me is death. Let's go back to America and have some fun." His smile widened as his sentence ended.

"Thank you," was all Casper muttered in response. Turning around, he stumbled right into a dirt path cutting through the jungle.

"Well look at that, you found the road." Poncho laughed as Casper led them along the side of the road, trying to stay hidden from any traffic that may pass by. Not long after they found the path, a small truck rumbled on, letting its lights blare in its passing. The three friends quickly took cover behind a group of tall ferns. It traveled noisily along, leaving the village and heading towards the airport. Seeing a sudden advantage, Casper took it. Leading the other two, he jumped on the rear fender, making sure to stay invisible to the driver.

Using the truck for transportation, they made it all the way to the airport in less time than Casper could have hoped for. Jumping off the vehicle while it was still in motion, they returned to hiding in the tree line before anyone could see the wanted hitch hikers. The airport runway was more closely guarded then the town and would seem that every inch of it was crawling with armed guards.

"Now what the hell are we suppose to do?" Casper asked quietly as he rubbed his back. Sore from the uncomfortable ride, he tried futilely to ease the aching.

"Hold on, I got an idea." Poncho whispered. "You just stay here." Before he could object to Poncho's maliciously grinning face, the agile boy was off running in a jagged pattern towards the fence that surrounded the run way.

"Damn I hope he's not doing something stupid." Casper grumbled to Isabella as the figure disappeared into darkness.

Sitting in the brush, they waited silently for Poncho to come back. They began to believe he would never return and had abandoned them, but after about half an hour they could hear gunshots, making them gasp in worrisome alarm. Their feelings were distracted however, for it soon turned to fear as some gargantuan creation could be seen heading towards them from the runway, destroying everything in its path and rapidly approaching the fence, only seconds from destroying the metallic blockade.

Chapter 21

Blaring lights brightened the jungle as the metal abomination approached them, crushing the fence in its path. Casper grabbed Isabella's arm and pulled her into a quick roll to the left, desperately trying to avoid being destroyed. As it cleared the fence and closed in on their location, Casper realized the large metallic object was actually a small airplane which was still being shot at by the guards. It turned sideways and an excited Poncho stuck his head out of the door.

"Get in, quick!" He yelled over the sound of the engines. Not having to be told twice, Casper pulled Isabella over to the passenger side of the plane. The personal aircraft was close to the ground and made it easy for them to leap in while avoiding stray bullets as they went. As soon as he heard the hatch close, Poncho used the controls to point the craft in the direction of a clear space. Getting as much running space as he could, he took flight.

Casper pushed Isabella roughly into a back seat where she hastily buckled up before he jumped into the co-pilot's chair. Watching the ground below them disappear, they all could see the guards shooting frantically at their craft, letting their gunshots pelt the plane. "This was your brilliant plan? Do you even know how to fly this thing?" Casper demanded, turning back to Poncho.

"Yeah, my dad taught me. He used to fly planes for the Harbieno overlords, before moving to America. He didn't have a piloting license, so had to get a job with Jesse."

"So you've flown before then?" Poncho turned and stared at Casper a moment with a nervous smile on his face.

"Yeah, but only on the ground. He never let me take off."

"Oh," Casper gripped the arm rests a little tighter, feeling slightly nauseous at his response. "Well what did your father carry in the planes?"

"He never said what it was, but we all knew whatever it was wasn't legal." Thoughts of what Enrique could have been transporting made Casper grimace and shudder.

"Wait, we've got to get back to Heresen," Casper said suddenly as he jumped up in alarm. "How the hell are we going to get past the American borders?"

"My father used to do it all the time." Without turning, Poncho responded nonchalantly to Casper's worried tone. "We just have to figure out how he did it." With that being said, the boy's face twisted in fake concentration, trying to avoid continuing the conversation.

"Great," Casper muttered, slumping back into his seat, "like any of us know how to avoid government radars."

"We a small aircraft," he answered after waiting a moment. "We fly low and out to sea. When we come back to shore, they think we're just a personal pilot and leave us alone."

"You think that'll work?" He asked, raising an eyebrow.

"Well we better hope so. I don't have any other ideas." He twisted the controls, forcing the plane to turn towards the western border of Mexico. "We going to America!" He called back to Isabella.

"America?" she giggled. "I have always wanted to go to America. It must be so beautiful!"

"Don't hold your breath," Casper huffed, thinking back to their destination in Heresen. They all looked out the windows into pitch darkness as Poncho guided the craft through the air and into the clouds.

"We will be safe up here until we in open waters," Poncho said with satisfaction. "The Harbieno overlords will not go to the Mexican government with this and by the time they send people after us, we will be long gone. Just as long as we stay out of anyone's view."

Casper could only nod at his pilot's response. What they were doing was risky but their choices were limited and at the moment he had no better plans. As hard as he tried, he couldn't help but let sleep overtake him as the plane floated through the night sky. Isabella was not far behind in dreams, leaving only Poncho awake to steer alone.

Fields stretched out in front of Isabella as her dainty toes dug into the fresh dirt underneath. Clover and lilacs filled the air with their sweet fragrances as a slight breeze made them dance in the wind. She giggled happily at the sight she saw before her. Clouds floated above her like giant pieces of cotton swimming in a blue sea. A soft chanting, intertwined with the wind, rested in her ears and soothed her very soul. Looking around, she tried to determine where the noise was coming from. Slight apprehension crossed her mind as she realized that nothing was in sight for miles in the vast fields.

Tuning in to concentrate on the song, she soon realized it was actually Poncho softly whispering somewhere nearby. She began walking through the grass, letting its lush green blades brush against her bare feet.

Looking down suddenly as she walked, she became aware of the clothes she wore and she marveled at the elaborate blue dress flowing against her body. Not knowing where it came from, she only knew that it was nothing like any one she had ever owned. It was, in fact, the most beautiful piece of clothing she had ever seen and she could only guess the value of it, though she supposed it still wouldn't come even close. She felt like a princess whose gorgeous countenance would be admired throughout America.

"Poncho!" She called out. "Poncho, where are you?" The soft singing continued as she ran about, fascinated by the world around her. The singing grew louder as she ran on, making her quicken her pace onwards. Before long she could see her love standing atop a small hill surrounded by roses. Dressed like a prince, he wore a stunning wardrobe made up of the finest pants and shirt she had ever seen. His bright red shirt was slit halfway down, letting the flaps of cloth fall open to reveal his masculine chest. The red cloth disappeared into the black pants around his legs that were neatly tucked into knee high boots made of black leather.

He stared blindly out, singing a strange song that she had never heard before. This only served to make her run even faster toward him, calling out desperately with each step.

"Poncho, I am here. I do not want to part with you again," despite her yelling, he only looked out into the empty fields, keeping in time with his soothing song. "Poncho, do you not miss me? You left me once do not do it again!" Tears welled in her eyes as she grabbed him around the waist, crying into his shoulder.

"Isabella," he stated, finally looking down with a smile. With his strong arms he embraced her against his chest. "We can be together, forever like this. No more worries for us, my love."

"What?" she asked, looking up with a confused look on her face. "What do you mean?"

"Do you not love this place?"

"Well yes," she started after a moment. "But where are we? Is this America?"

"It's wherever you want it to be, my love. We can be free here for the rest of our lives. No one will tell us what to do or make us work."

"That sounds wonderful." Breathing deeply, she let the soft scents of her surroundings encompass her before continuing. "I would like that very much."

"Good. Only one thing stands in our way from true happiness. His name is Casper."

"Casper? But he is our friend. Why would he not want us to be happy?"

"Casper is a bad man. All we have to do is bring him to people who will take care of him for us."

"He is not bad." Isabella looked at her love with a perplexing stare. "He is trying to help us."

"No he is not. He is saving you for a sacrifice. Once we get back to America he will use you to give himself more power. He only cares about you because you are useful to him."

"That is not true!" she yelled up at him, tears streaming down her cheeks. "He is our friend and keeps both of us safe. Why do you want to get rid of him?"

"He will betray us. You must believe me. I heard him talking to someone the other night. He told them all about his elaborate plans to sacrifice you to them. I do not want to lose you. I want us to be happy forever."

"Liar! I will not trust you. You are not Poncho! Who are you?" She pushed away from his warm embrace as the air turned cold. Bright blue skies turned dark and grey as lightning streaked its bolts across the menacing clouds.

"You will help us." A snake like tongue protruded from Poncho's mouth and hung there, free to whip around in the breeze which grew stronger with each gust. Isabella had to brace herself so as to not be blown away by the wild wind. As the air threatened to tear her from the spot, the green grass dissipated between her toes, leaving only bare, cracked earth in its place. Its hard surface felt cold against her feet, making her gasp as she tried to back away from the creature in front of her. His face twisted and distorted grotesquely until it was beyond any possible recognition.

"Stop it!" she yelled, trying to cut through the wind with her voice. "You're scaring me!"

"You want me to stop?" the voice no longer came from his mouth, but instead seemed to haunt her mind. "Then you will give us the cyspherion!" As he spoke, tendrils sprouted from his midsection, aiming for her face with the intent of causing her pain. "Or you will suffer our wrath!"

"No!" Her hands shot to her head as she screamed, protecting it from the oncoming menace as she backed up. Not paying attention to where she was going, her legs tripped over themselves, making her fall onto her back, where she pulled herself into a feeble ball of protection. "Just leave me alone!"

Her shouts rang through the small airplane. Even with the loud roar of the engines, Casper and Poncho could hear her yelling in the back seat. Turning around, Casper looked back with a concerned stare. Poncho, momentarily distracted, looked back as well but realized he was still piloting and turned around to concentrate on the skies.

"What is wrong?" he shouted back, trying to divide his attention between flying and his girlfriend. "Are you alright, my love?" Worry streaked his questions as the confused boy yelled over the engine's roar.

"Nothing, I am fine. It was just a bad dream." She called back. Unable to convince even herself that it had been just a nightmare, she wondered if they believed her. Casper shrugged as he turned back to Poncho, talking in a low tone to him. She couldn't make out his words so let her mind drift back to her previous thoughts. What if someone was after them? She didn't want to see Casper get hurt as he was their friend and would protect them from harm.

She turned to look through the window at her side. Looking down, she could see the moon reflecting off of the waves far below. They had made it out of Mexico without a problem, but she still wondered if they would make it over the American border safely. If not, at least Casper and Poncho would protect her from harm. Turning back, she eyed Casper, who stared out the front of the plane. His weathered shirt hung loosely on his muscular chest. Still torn down the center, it resembled a peasant's clothing, stained with blood from being impaled with his own weapons. His dirt-encrusted pants were no better and his skin shone through their ragged panels while they barely covered his legs. His dirty feet were no longer protected as his shoes had been destroyed and thrown aside somewhere in the jungle. The only article of clothing still in good repair was his sturdy belt, which had miraculously withstood the tribulations of the jungle.

"Where is your swords Casper?" Staring at his belt, she saw that they no longer hung inside the sheaths. In fact, the sheaths themselves had disappeared all together.

"Huh, What?" His hands shot down to his waist, where his belt was as he snapped his head back toward Isabella. "They're right here," he responded, pulling the two blades from thin air.

"How did you do that?"

"Do what?" Confusion from the tiny girl's voice made him pause. He looked down at his waist, searching for the sheaths that were seemingly invisible. He rested his swords against the seat and felt around to find that the two pieces of leather still on his belt. Sliding the blades inside, he stared in fascination as they disappeared out of sight.

"They must be enchanted," He surmised as the hilts themselves vanished between his bent knuckles. "The scabbards must make them invisible to the human eye." Thinking back, Casper realized he had not paid too close attention to the blades while they were at his side. He had memorized their locations and never bothered to examine them or their scabbards while they were sheathed.

"But why could we see the scabbards before?"

"They must need someone… or something to wear them first." He played with the invisible objects, amazed at the magic behind them. "I just wished Jasselbad had warned me about them first. Well it's going to at least make walking around in public a hell of a lot easier."

"Land!" Poncho's yell surprised both of them. They turned back toward the cockpit, searching for the alleged land. Barely visibly in the darkness was a coastline, with its beaches illuminated by the moon which had begun to set, making the world outside their plane harder to see.

"You've done excellent." Casper mused, putting his hand on the pilot's shoulder. "Now let's see if you can get us back to Heresen."

"I will Casper, I will."

•~~~~~~~~~~~~~~•~~~~~~~~~~~~~~•

"You are requested to land immediately!" A young man's voice buzzed over the plane's radio, snapping them to attention. "I repeat, land immediately. You are in restricted air space. Failure to comply will result in being dealt with extreme prejudice." The two men in the cockpit stared at each other. The sun had only just begun rising on a new day and they had already made a decent way across land. Behind them loomed two jets from the American Air Force.

"I don't think they want us around." Casper groaned.

"What we going to do?"

"This is your final warning. Land immediately or face the consequences." Casper stared at the box making the noises in front of him for just a moment before grabbing the communication device.

"What exactly does that entail?" Casper questioned, pushing the button to speak and cringing at his obvious question.

After a static pause, the man on the other end replied. "We will gun you down."

"Isn't that a little drastic? Can't you just let us pass through? We're on our way home and we're in a hurry."

"You must land so we can verify your information. Terrorist threats are on the rise and we are willing to take no chances."

"But our grandmother is dying. We have no idea how long she has left to live." Casper forced sobs into his lie, trying to make it all the more believable. "We have to go see her before then, we promised her."

"Land now, or be prepared to crash." The static cut out as Casper threw the radio's microphone angrily at the control panel.

"How good are you at flying evasive maneuvers?" He asked, turning back to Poncho.

A sullen look crossed his face as he began to bring the plane towards the ground in a landing position.

"We can't just give up. There's no way they're going to just let us go!" Casper yelled at him as they rapidly approached the earth with the two jets in tow.

Poncho waited until the jets were prepared to land before pulling all the way back on the controls, pulling the small plane skywards at terrifying speeds. "Looks like we find out just how good I am." He responded as the sullen look turned into a smile.

The jets down below reacted quickly, working to get their crafts in the air. Their machine guns started blazing with their deadly metal bullets. With the jets' turrets aimed at their plane, Poncho did all he could to avoid the flying projectiles. He avoided most of them but could only do so much and heard as some of them zinging by as they ripped holes in the plane's metal.

"Stop shooting please!" Casper yelled over the radio as the bullets surrounded them, making it hard for Poncho to steer. No response came over from the other flyers. Hanging up the radio, he looked back to Poncho's right wing. Something looked wrong with the jet flying nearby there. Even though he was well in range and surely had not run out of ammunition, its machine gun had stopped shooting at them. Squinting to see better, Casper realized just a little too late what the following jet was doing.

"Missiles on your right side!" He yelled just as the rockets left the jet's wing and followed the death path aimed straight for them. A terrible roar resounded through the cabin as one missile hit dead on, making the unprotected aircraft fall into a tailspin. Two more missiles found their mark on the plane's back, dislodging the wings completely and taking away any little bit of control Poncho had over the craft.

"We going to crash!" Poncho screamed as realization struck that he could no longer pilot the vessel. The ground below them came closer and closer as the three friends released their safety harnesses. Pushing themselves out of their seats, they all huddled into a ball as they flew towards the back of the plane, trying to shelter one another from the impending collision.

Chapter 22

The ground loomed just a few hundred feet below, making them all the more scared of crashing into it. Stuck to the back of the plane by the force of the fall, they whispered prayers of safety just before plowing into the dirt and grass. In a final attempt to save them before impact, Casper's subconscious mind radiated a ball of white light around them. It took the brunt of the fall, making them grunt slightly as they fell rapidly from the back of the plane to the cockpit, still trapped in the ball of white light. Releasing his spell, Casper pushed his way to the hatch which he had to kick open to breathe in the fresh open air outside. As they stumbled out into the cool morning air, each one looked up to see the jets descending on their location.

"We need to get out of here," Casper said, snapping all three out of a trance and causing them all to run away from the wreck. Looking around desperately as they ran, each one searched for a means to hide from the jets, only to find that all about them was a vast field of wheat. Tripping through the tall vegetation, they sped anxiously away as the sounds of the jets loomed nearby, coming closer with every passing second.

Just as they heard the jet engines cut out just behind them, they stumbled upon a path. However ill maintained it was, it still resembled a dirt road of sorts and down it just a little ways shimmered civilization in the form of a city. Only taking a second to look at it before running blindly forward, the three sprinted with all their strength to escape the pursuers.

Luckily for them, the city was within running distance and despite the sun beating down on them, it didn't slow down the trio by much. Any idea of the United State's army chasing the fugitives only made them run even faster. The pilots, who had stopped to inspect the wreckage, lagged far behind and had just found the dirt road just as Casper, Poncho and Isabella reached the city limits.

"Where do we go now?" Isabella asked, out of breath from running. "I can not run anymore." She stopped and put her hands on her knees, panting uncontrollably.

"Over there." They all looked to the shopping center Casper pointed vigorously to. "They won't find us in the mall!"

"Casper," Poncho protested as the cyspherion pushed them closer to his destination. "It like eighty degrees out here and there's not a cloud in the sky right now. No one going to be in the mall. We will be like sitting ducks."

"Don't count on it." Casper grinned as they reached the glass doors. "If I remember correctly it should be Saturday."

"So?" As the glass doors opened, a whoosh of cold air flowed out onto their faces. Poncho stopped resisting when he looked inside. The mall was crowded with shoppers all looking discontent and bored as they walked around indecisively. He gaped at the mere number of people before plunging in just behind Casper, holding Isabella's hand.

They were soon lost in a swarm of arrogant mall rats that came merely to pass time or pretend to be a better person than those stuck behind the registers. Casper scowled at each human as they passed by, watching them give mall workers a hard time or being unnecessarily loud and obnoxious.

Looking down at their own clothes, they felt suddenly out of place in the tattered rags that stuck to their skin. They swiftly and quietly shuffled into the nearest clothing store. As they passed by racks, nonchalant hands reached out and grabbed the closest articles of clothing until they reached the changing rooms. They each took a booth and quickly donned their new found apparel, hiding the old cloth inconspicuously under the seats of the changing booths before looking at themselves in the mirror. The only thing that they bothered keeping was Casper's belt, which held his two beloved swords against his waist.

With careful inspection, each one plucked sales tags from their attire to ensure they wouldn't be detected before emerging and meeting the rest of the group. After they were finished, the thieving trio walked quietly out of the store, evading every suspicious eye to avoid being caught.

After blending into the crowd for a few minutes, they came to the mall's overly crowded food court. Delicious aromas wafted from every direction as they forced their way through the thick crowd. While inspecting the eateries, they realized that a most peculiar sight was happening within a donut shop standing on the corner of court. A man Casper gauged to be around twenty three and dressed like a professional manager was actually fighting with a customer. A much smaller and chubbier aged woman stood across the counter from him. He couldn't quite make out the words, but could see the foam cup in their hands that was being fought over. As he made his way curiously over, Casper could begin to hear what they were saying.

"But ma'am, its twenty five cents for the cup." The worker protested.

"I don't care. I should get it for free. I need the water and you need to give it to me," she fired back, pulling even harder on the foam cup.

"Everyone needs to pay for the cups. It costs us too much money to give them away free." He attempted to pull the cup free from her grasp as he spoke.

"It's only a cup," she screeched. Finally pulling it free from him, she stumbled off and waddled proudly away.

"What the hell was that all about?" Seeing there was no line, Casper edged up to the register and inquired about the recent incidents.

"That woman wanted a cup of water," he replied with a sigh. "They all want free cups. It costs us too much money, so we started charging for them."

"Makes sense to me," Casper bit his lip, thinking for a second. "Why did you let her have it then? Didn't seem like you were giving too much of a struggle."

"It was filled with hot water. If it spilled onto her hand, she would've come back and sued us."

Casper thought about it for responding. "I see. Get a lot of customers like that?"

"More than you know."

Casper nodded but his response was cut off by Poncho and Isabella, who came running quickly to his side. Grabbing his hands, they pulled him anxiously away from the food counter, to the surprise of the man standing behind it.

"What's going on?" He demanded as they dragged him to the window of an electronic store, but soon realized what they were so worried about. Inside the window a brand new high definition television buzzed with a newscast.

"Still at large is Casper Michael Maverick." She proclaimed. "Last seen at the Heresen airport, he is considered extremely dangerous and should not be approached if seen on the streets. Please contact local authorities as soon as possible," She continued as a poorly filmed video of Casper appeared on the screen. "This is a video taken from the airport cameras two months ago. He is wanted for numerous crimes including vandalism of Heresen's streets, disturbing of the peace, the kidnapping of Poncho Ranchesco," as she said his name, a picture of Poncho appeared on screen with his name underneath. "And the murder of numerous citizens."

Casper had heard enough. Grabbing the children by their wrists, he ducked between the crowds, trying to avoid attention as he darted between the grungy people filling up the space in the mall. He bolted over to an escalator bringing its passengers upwards to the mall's second floor. Without thinking twice, he pushed his way onto it, letting Poncho and Isabella climb on behind.

As the moving staircase began its descent upwards, he noted that the escalator to the left of him was carrying people downwards. He watched them with disinterest until a gap appeared in the crowd. A small girl stood on a step alone with no one around to accompany her. She may have been little, but Casper guessed she had to be at least eighteen. Her small frame was adorned with jeans and a t shirt depicting some sort of a rock band on its front. She had the blondest hair Casper had ever seen draping over a brooding face. Her looks, accented with arms across her chest, told him that there was something peculiar about this girl.

He had never been in love, but he suddenly had the urge to find out what it was like. It was the girl he had always dreamed of but could never find. While he stared hopelessly at her beautifully green eyes, they rolled over to his part of the escalator. They passed each other, sharing a glance and a smile, before the stairs took them away from each other. Casper turned in desperation to jump over the escalator wall only to be stopped when Poncho grabbed him by the shoulder and firmly held the man back.

"Wait," Poncho commanded as he pointed down the stairs. "We need to get out of here, quickly." Casper followed Poncho's finger to where a few security guards were gathering. "Apparently they saw you on the news too." One guard pointed vigorously up the stairs, excited to be on the chase. The others started piling onto the escalator, roughly forcing people out of their way as they climbed to the top.

"Come on, we need to find a way out, quickly!" They reached the top of the escalator to where a few brave souls had decided to block their escape from the escalator. Without caring, Casper shoulder rammed the men creating the chain and immediately began running down the packed mall's second floor. Poncho grabbed Isabella's hand once more and began chasing him down, trying his best to keep up with his rampaging friend.

If anyone got in Casper's way, he rudely pushed them away and continued his frantic search for a means of escape. Everywhere he turned there loomed a guard prepared to apprehend the three and the mall seemed to stretch on forever, making them slow down the pace rapidly as their energy ran out.

Just as they thought they couldn't run any longer, the three of them came upon a presentation at the end of the second floor. New cars lined the mall hallways in attempts to pique customer's interest in buying them from a new dealership down the street. The closest vehicle to them was a shining new black Proviac blazewing. Casper gasped in its beauty. He had always dreamed of having one, but knew he could never own it personally. Its body swooped down in perfect curves all the way to the spoiler on the edge of the hatchback. The interior was upholstered with black leather and The roof was made in the fashion of removable panels, making it easily into a roadster. The car sat low, only a few inches from the ground. Its engine was a powerhouse mystery, containing an engine unknown to the general public on how components worked. The only information they knew was that it used no fuel but instead was able to run efficiently without.

"I've got an idea," Casper said quickly as he ran to the blazewing's side. With a quick tug he pulled the door open and hit the unlock button. "Get in!" Casper yelled as he climbed into the driver's seat. Poncho pulled Isabella to the car door and opened it, pushing her quickly in before jumping in himself. Casper searched frantically around the front of the car as Poncho slammed the door.

"What you doing?" He asked, turning back towards where Casper sat.

"Looking for the keys, they're not in the ignition!"

"Check the ashtray and hurry." As Casper scrambled for the ashtray, he looked out the windshield to see a rather large group of security guards running for the car, making him search even faster. Flipping it open, a pair of metallic keys jingled about, free of their hiding place in the dashboard. He grabbed them up and shoved one into the ignition. Twisting it quickly, he heard the engine turn over and start up.

"Wait. How they get these cars up here anyway?" Poncho asked, suddenly aware that they were still on the second floor.

"Beats me, better question is do you really trust me driving when I've never done it before?" Poncho and Isabella looked at each other in sudden fear. With a lunge, they both dove for the doors in attempts to unlock them. "Too late." He muttered as his finger pressed the locking button on his side control panel. Smiling as he heard the door's mechanical locks engage, he grabbed the shifter and pulled it into drive. With a mighty stomp, he pushed the pedal to the floor, listening as the car squealed its tires on the tiles, trying to find traction on the slippery surface. Finally catching, the blazewing lurched forward, throwing everyone back into their seats. Customers roaming the mall leapt hurriedly out of its way as it sped off, creating a passage in its wake. The guards saw the opportunity and used the passage to chase the car down the mall as it drove away from them.

Casper watched as a giant window appeared at the other end of the mall, just in front of the car. Running out of space to go, Casper had to make a quick decision. Isabella screamed as glass shattered around them. The window gave little resistance as they sailed out into open air. A full parking lot lay just beneath their tires that spun frantically, free of the mall's floor. The window's broken glass followed them through the hole, crashing down and shattering onto the ground down below.

Isabella's scream lasted all the way to the ground, where the excellent suspension of the blazewing took the brutal impact as they it landed in between a row of cars. Once the tires met with the pavement, they let out a terrifying screech and left two trails of rubber behind them as he sped off. With obvious difficulties, Casper navigated through the parking lot, almost hitting several pedestrians that walked blindly in his way. He swerved out of the way of one woman as she crossed the pavement, not bothering to look where she was going as she pushed a baby carriage right in his way. As he spun the steering wheel to the right to avoid the carriage, he was forced to scrape the paint off of a nearby car. Turning the wheel back to the left sharply, he narrowly averted broad-siding a vehicle as it pulled out of its parking space. With another stomp on the pedal, they lurched out of the parking lot and into the street. Leaving the mall at frightening speeds, Casper tried to put as much distance between them and the mall as possible.

Chapter 23

Sirens screeched somewhere behind the blazewing as it tore down the road. The small car maneuvered perfectly around a corner as if it were made specifically for this purpose. Turning a full one hundred and eighty degrees, Casper drove the way they had just come and winced as the sounds of the police cruisers drew closer.

"Where you going?" Poncho yelled from the back seat. "You bringing us back to the cops!"

"I know but we're in Faulkland though. I recognize that mall now." He swerved the wheel quickly to the right, just making the ramp for the highway. "This will take us to Ravenport. Then we can take the forty five south back to Heresen." He sped aggressively around the ramp and onto the highway. Merging, he made his way all the way to the left lane.

Police cars came down the highway and quickly found the stolen car as it headed northbound. Turning around at a connecting point, they began following him closely, making Casper worry a little. He turned the car sharply, merging back into the middle lane and cutting off a van. As the closest two cop cars tried to follow in pursuit, they cut off too early and collided with the van, causing a momentary roadblock. They could hear the sound of metal crashing as they drove off, slaloming through the light traffic in the way.

"Casper…" A short whimper came from Isabella as she stared uneasily forward. "Casper…"

"What?"

"I have got to use the bathroom." She whined as she started bouncing up and down in the seat.

"Can't you hold it? We're a little busy right now."

"No, I have to go really bad."

"Those cops are going to be right behind us!" His patience started growing short. "Stopping now could cost us our lives!"

"Casper!" Poncho shot back sternly. "None of us have used the bathroom in a while. We could all use a break. Besides, that sign says there a rest area just ahead. They will not be expecting us to be there and it will be off the road. They will never find us. We can lay low until they gone." Grunting in agreement, Casper realized that they all could use a break. He watched the sign go by saying there would be a rest area within one mile. He roughly swerved to the right and waited for the road to split off. The car slowed down to a halt as they pulled into the parking area. With a quick push, he slid the gears from drive to park, stopping noisily in a parking spot.

"Alright, let's go, everybody out!" He shouted to the back, waving his arm to the building at the end of the lot. "Let's go!" Without having to be told twice, Isabella opened the door with a great push, letting the outside air rush in.

"Race you!" she laughed, pushing Poncho down in the seat before jumping out of the car and running towards the rest area. He quickly jumped back up, ready to get back in the race until Casper put his arm firmly onto his shoulder.

"She's a good girl," He said, pointing toward the girl as she continued running, oblivious to what was happening in the car. "I can see why you went all the way back to Mexico for her. Just don't lose her again." As he finished, his eyes turned serious as they gazed deeply into Poncho's.

"I won't," he promised.

Just as the two looked back up to where Isabella was running, a drakengol jumped from the nearby bushes surrounding the building. With dread on their lips, they shouted in alarm, watching as it bounded swiftly towards the helpless girl. Poncho pulled the machete free from its hiding place under his new clothes. Casper felt around until his knuckles gripped the sword hilts at his side. As he began to draw the blades, he heard police cruisers come into the parking lot with lights and sirens blaring. His eyes snapped to the back window at the sound of the police entering but the sound of Isabella screaming as she was abducted brought him back to reality.

"We can't take them all on," he surmised aloud. "Go save Isabella!" He reached back and grabbed Poncho's shoulder, pushing the already armed boy out of the car door. "I'm going to distract the rest!" As Poncho jumped out of the door, he paused only a moment to push the door closed with his foot before running off. Casper watched as Poncho sped off and waited just long enough to see him disappear into the bushes that the drakengol had pulled Isabella into.

Cops pulled all around Casper as he forced the shifter back into drive. Not wanting to waste any more time, he floored the pedal, taking back off and leaving the police force behind. He pushed the blazewing harder when he saw them fall back into pursuit. He tried not to leave them too far behind while they all drove back onto the highway.

"Come on, damn it," he muttered to himself as he drove faster. "Follow me, not them. I'm the guy you want." His eyes darted up while he spoke, letting him see the Ravenport exit just ahead of him. The three of them had made more progress than he originally thought and he was now just about to enter Ravenport. He watched the exit pass by, letting himself run into the right lane as he went. Just after he passed the exit ramp he pushed the brakes hard, screeching to a halt. Smiling, he watched the cops fly by him while he spun the wheel all the way to the right. Stomping the gas pedal again, he drove onto the exit median and drove the car back onto the exit. Driving roughly, he made his way into the city. The cops were quick to realize what had happened and were already turning their cars back around. They were soon in Ravenport, chasing Casper as he drove on.

The forty five south's exit came up quick. As he slowed down, the cops failed to fall for another of his tricks. They drove ahead, ready to block his way. Two cars moved to block the main road while one car blocked the ramp. Laughing maliciously, Casper drove up the ramp, staying all the way to the left, he still clipped the trunk of the cop car blocking the ramp. He felt a slight bump as impact shook his car and pushed the cop out of the way. The left side of Casper's car scraped against a jersey barrier as he drove on, pushing the engine harder to escape the scene.

Red reached across the sky as the sun set, leaving Casper in shadowed twilight while he made his way south on the highway. The drive from Ravenport to Heresen usually takes only a couple of minutes, but with the accelerated rate of Casper's stolen blazewing, he was there in less than three. While speeding onto the exit ramp, three police cruisers closed in from behind.

"Must be state forces," he grunted, leaning into the sharp turn as he drove around the ramp and into Heresen. Turning back forward, he came suddenly upon a tractor trailer parked perpendicular to him in the middle of the road.

"Damn!" Staying on track, he sped even faster towards the parked truck, listening as the police cruisers followed closely behind, ready to apprehend him as soon as he stopped. With what little running space that was left, he let the car go to full speed and just as the nose of his car plummeted under the truck's midsection, he drew a deep breath. Swiftly reaching down he pulled the chair's reclining lever up and pushed seat all the way down until he was lying perfectly horizontal. Just as his seat touched the end of its track, he heard heavy metal grinding. Sparks flew all about him as the trailer took his roof off, tearing it roughly from the car's body. The top of the car crushed against the truck's gigantic side, falling uselessly behind him as Casper closed his eyes to avoid shrapnel from getting into them. The rest of the car emerged on the other side. Realizing that he had made it through in one piece, he pulled the reclining lever back up and looked around with slight shock.

"Convertible," he huffed with disappointment. "I had my dream car for one day and it's already wrecked." Keeping his foot on the pedal, he continued quickly away as the pursuing cars crashed violently into the trailer's side, causing a ferocious fireball in their explosions.

He smiled evilly at the gruesome sounds as he surveyed the town around the car. His smile turned into a state of shock while a dry feeling clung to the back of his throat. All around him the town was destroyed and deserted. Buildings and cars burned, lighting up the night air and casting shadows upon the faces of a few desolate souls roaming the streets. Judging by the state they were in, Casper guessed that they had been homeless for some time. Slowing down, he observed the horrendous sight in anger and awe. He drove by Beezel's and groaned in disgust as black smoke rose from his favorite bar.

He wasn't sure what madness had befallen his town, but he was certain Wyburn could tell him. Driving slowly about, he made his way back to his house. Stopping the car just in front of it, he got out and slammed the door. A sigh escaped his lips as he looked at the smoking domicile. Even though it was in better repair at this point than most of Heresen, it was still more dilapidated than how he had left it.

"Casper!" Preparing to go in, he heard a voice he had not heard in over two months. His face grew angry as he turned, resting his hands on the sword hilts.

"Wyburn…" he hissed at the approaching figure. No longer masked in his disguise as a human, he strode proudly forward while his silvery white wings scraped the ground behind him. Dressed in chainmail from his head to his feet, Casper could tell he was prepared for battle.

"You killed my mother you bastard!" He yelled across the street towards the figure. "I will avenge her death!"

"I did what I had to do," he replied sternly. "There's not a day that goes by where I don't regret what I've done. Let the past be in the past." As he spoke, he walked closer and closer, finally meeting Casper on the sidewalk where he stood.

"That's no excuse. I never even knew her and you took her away from me." Casper's voice lowered, but the feeling of disdain stayed as he stared the lesser angel in the eye. "What happened here?" His words hissed out of his mouth as he leaned closer. "This destruction has your stench all over it."

"A war has been called out. When you left, you took your magic with you. The barriers on the Wrokthien portals deteriorated and allowed safe passage for any magical being. With false confidence, both Zeus and Satan sprung into action, sending in counterattacks on each other. No longer wanting to abide by the laws, they felt they could defy GOD and attack without rules, destroying the town as a result." He paused for a second, letting Casper grasp exactly what had happened. He merely stared back with a rock hard face, listening to Wyburn's story. "The survivors of Heresen are left confused and homeless. No one told them about magical creatures and so they were never introduced to it." Casper's face flickered with a slight confusion. He looked on, trying to figure out exactly what Wyburn was getting at. Wyburn, catching sight of Casper's confusion, stopped to explain in further detail.

"Magic tends to stay hidden for normal humans. It's the law of GOD. A person must be introduced to magic for it to appear normally. This helps to keep most humans safe from its harm. With the attack of Heresen though, no one was safe." As he spoke, he waved his arm around, motioning to the city about them. "Now there's no time. Zeus' armies are weak, but Satan's are even weaker. With you leading us we can end this once and for all. Follow me!" He turned around, waving for Casper to follow him.

"All I care to end," Casper growled as he slowly freed the blades from their invisible sheaths, "Is your life!" He ended his sentence with a yell as he thrust blades into a crossed pattern just at the back of Wyburn's exposed neck. "Any last words before I kill you, murderer?" He sneered, pressing the metal against Wyburn's neck.

"Casper! There you are!" The sound of Jesse's voice caused Casper to lose sight of what he was doing. Loosening his tension the swords, he turned to see Jesse running from his house. "Where have you been?"

"I explain it all later!" He yelled. Turning back, he became aware that Wyburn had taken the opportunity of distraction and escaped his scissor-like threat, disappearing somewhere down the road. "Damn," he moaned to himself. "Where's Justine, is she safe?"

A sorrowful look crossed Jesse's face as he slowed his run to a halt next to him. "I'm sorry. They came last night..." A tear appeared in the corner of his eye as he spoke. "I fended them off as long as I could. They weren't even human..."

"What were they?" Casper's rough voice cut him off as he spoke.

"I don't know. I've never seen them before. They were shrouded in black, like assassins or ninjas or something. And they moved like a weasels."

"Drakengols," he hissed back.

"They were led by Ben. He said something about ruling a part of earth and being able to choose his own queen."

"Where did they bring her?" Casper could feel his anger rising and already could feel flames ready to come to life.

"They headed towards Beezel's. I couldn't follow them in the dark. I searched all today but couldn't find them anywhere."

"Go home, get your gun. Meet me back at Beezel's." Jesse nodded. He knew exactly which gun Casper was talking about. A belt-fed gun turret that was originally mounted on an old attack copter that had been discharged from service, Jesse had modified it to be a somewhat portable minigun, even though Jesse was one of the only ones strong enough to wield it. Turning quickly, Jesse ran off in the direction of his house.

"She's already lost to you!" Wyburn reappeared from around the broken blazewing as Jesse sprinted off. "I know you're mad at me and at Ben, but killing either one of us won't help you. The only way to save yourself is to come help out Zeus in a final battle."

Looking back with a new rage, Casper glared at the majestic angel, ready to rend him apart with either sword. "I'll deal with you later, old man!" The cyspherion hissed as he turned around toward the bar. Red eyes glinted in the night as he walked away from Wyburn, stepping in and out of the rolling smoke. The only noise Wyburn could hear from the figure as he walked away was the sound of metal against metal as he slid his twin swords across each other.

"Foolish boy," Wyburn growled with disdain to his back before turning and walking swiftly the other way.

High above, Sheila gave out a mighty shriek as clouds wisped away from her wings. Jasselbad sat on her back with his battleaxe held high. War was on the horizon and he knew it wouldn't be long before he was contracted to fight. As they glided high above, Sheila's sharp eyes caught movement on the ground below.

"Get back!" Justine screeched at her captors. She had cut loose her bindings and made it out onto the street before the drakengols had discovered her escape. Gripping a pipe tightly in her hands, she swung ferociously at the deformed creatures as they hissed all around her. Her rage filled shrieks caught Casper's attention from down the street.

The song of metal filled the air as an unsuspecting drakengol fell helplessly to the ground. Standing behind him, the angered cyspherion retracted his deadly blades.

"Let's play," he growled as the others looked on in alarm. The closest one snapped out of his trance and sprung for Casper's throat. As he approached him, Casper thrust out his left blade, letting its force drive itself onto the metal and down to his hand. With a quick flick of his wrist, he threw the body into another one, knocking her over from where she stood. "Miss me?" he asked, turning back to Justine.

"Hell yeah, Where you been?" She swung the pipe, landing a blow on a drakengol's shoulder and driving him onto the ground.

"On vacation." His right hand swung its blade, slashing a drakengol through the chest and making his upper torso slide off of his lower body. Spinning back around, he heard the one that had been knocked to the ground was beginning to stir. He heard a muffled girl's scream as he leapt towards the fallen body, landing in a crouch and driving both blades into the creature's body. A scream was let out as the monster writhed in pain under the twin blades. Standing back up, a gruesome sound followed the blades as he pushed his foot against the body and pulled them free of the body. Turning back around he was shocked to find there was no longer anyone else around.

"Justine?" His eyes darted around frantically, looking for his best friend. "Justine!" The sound of his voice echoed down the empty streets until it was lost on the cool winds.

Be ready for the second installment of the Painryte Chronicles:

Fractal Rose

The sound of sirens echoed throughout the otherwise quiet streets. A small girl clutched a teddy bear tightly to her chest as tears poured down her dirt streaked face. Branches pushed against her bare skin as she tried as hard as possible not to move in the lush underbrush of the hedges.

The sounds of yelling started to break through the raindrops, making her sniffle. The people searching for her weren't her real parents. Though she didn't know who they were exactly, her muddled mind could remember that much at least.

"Alexandria, Alexandria!" the five year old cringed every time she heard her name. It was as if they were tearing her soul apart. All they were after was her mind. They constantly lied to her, telling her that she was theirs. She knew they were trying to deceive her, but could no longer even remember who her real family was.

A black shoe scraped by the hedge and Alexandria used all of her restraint not to spit on it. It belonged to the man who claimed to be her father, Carl. He was the one who forced her to wear wrist bands constantly. She was never allowed to expose the skin to the world. She had gotten so used to them though that they barely even itched her anymore but thinking about it made her reach down and scratch them on impulse. If she could even remember correctly, the dirty clothing hid tattoos that had somehow become imprinted into her flesh. Whatever they were, they at least held some bearing as to where she had originally come from.

A mixed plethora of thoughts rolled through her head and though she tried as hard as possible, Alexandria could no longer distinguish the truth from the lies. After five years of repression, all that she knew for sure was that it was not her family she lived with and her only friend in the world was a shaggy teddy bear that she took with her everywhere.

The sounds of the search party faded and Alexandria heaved a sigh of relief. With one hand she gently rubbed rain drops from her eyes before using it to brace against the ground. With careful motions, she pushed her head through the front of the bush, checking to see if the coast was clear. A Street light illuminated the dark road, revealing no souls aside from herself. She tried to turn and look down the street but panic ripped through her body as a dog barked wildly. She instinctively pushed herself back into the prickly hiding spot and cried at how close an encounter she had just witnessed.

"Gotcha!" The muscles in her body had just relaxed when a meaty hand slammed into her chest and clenched into a firm grip around her shirt. The man outside the bush dragged her helplessly back out as she flailed and cried out in terror. Carl had her back in his control and there was nothing she could do.